# THE POSITION OF THE BODY

Books by Richard Stern

GOLK
EUROPE, OR UP AND DOWN WITH BAGGISH AND SCHREIBER
IN ANY CASE (reissued as THE CHALEUR NETWORK)
TEETH, DYING AND OTHER MATTERS
STITCH
HONEY AND WAX
1968. A SHORT NOVEL, AN URBAN IDYLL, FIVE STORIES AND
    TWO TRADE NOTES
OTHER MEN'S DAUGHTERS
THE BOOKS IN FRED HAMPTON'S APARTMENT
NATURAL SHOCKS
PACKAGES
THE INVENTION OF THE REAL
A FATHER'S WORDS
THE POSITION OF THE BODY

# THE POSITION OF THE BODY
Richard Stern

*Northwestern University Press*

*Evanston, Illinois*

Northwestern University Press, Evanston, Illinois 60201
© 1986 by Richard Stern
All rights reserved. Published 1986


Printed in the United States of America

Library of Congress Cataloging in Publication Data

Stern, Richard G., 1928–
  The position of the body.

  I. Title.
PS3569.T39P6   1986                809                86-16382
ISBN 0-8101-0730-9
ISBN 0-8101-0731-7 (pbk.)

Some essays in this collection have appeared in different form in the following: *Chicago, Chicago Review, The Daily News, Formations, Saturday Review, Sewanee Review, Shenandoah, Chicago Sun-Times, New York Times,* and the *Chicago Tribune.*

Grateful acknowledgment is made to Lawrence Toynbee for permission to reprint Arnold Toynbee's letter to Richard Stern.

*This book—and much besides—is dedicated to Liza Cady Baron, who has already taught her grandfather much about transmission and transfiguration.*

# CONTENTS

# Contents

*It will perhaps be objected to our opinion, that a man, for instance, being thought erect when his feet are next the earth, and inverted when his head is next the earth, it does hence follow that, by the mere act of vision, without any experience or altering the situation of the eye, we should have determined whether he were erect or inverted. For both the earth itself, and the limbs of the man who stands thereon, being equally perceived by sight, one cannot choose seeing what part of the man is nearest the earth, and what part farthest from it, i.e., whether he be erect or inverted.*

    *—Berkeley,* An Essay Toward a New Theory of Vision


*I know I am seated, my hands on my knees, because of the pressure against my rump, against the soles of my feet, against the palms of my hands, against my knees. Against my palms the pressure is of my knees, against my knees of my palms, but what is it that presses against my rump, against the soles of my feet? I don't know. My spine is not supported. I mention these details to make sure I am not lying on my back, my legs raised and bent, my eyes closed. It is well to establish the position of the body from the outset, before passing on to more important matters.*

    *—Beckett,* The Unnamable


*In health we always know where our bodies are and what position or posture we are in, and we know this without having to look and see where we, our trunk, our head, our limbs, are. The knowledge is . . . dependent on a specific sense, which was discovered in the 1890s by the British neurologist Charles Sherrington, who called it "our secret sense, our sixth sense" and named it proprioception because of its indispensability for our sense of ourselves.*

    *—Charles Rycroft. Review of Oliver Sacks,* The Man Who Mistook His Wife for a Hat and Other Clinical Tales

# PREFATORY NOTE

*The Position of the Body* is the third book of its kind I've published. "Its kind" is what I call an "orderly miscellany." The first book, *The Books in Fred Hampton's Apartment* (1973), began with a "defense of the miscellany." It wasn't "a grab-bag, waste-basket, office sweepings, old files, throat-clearings, leftovers, hash, rubble or a hotel for transients." The negatives were a defense. As for what the book was, I suggested bouillabaisse, the Plaza, and such collections of odd pieces as the *Arabian Nights*, the Greek and Confucian anthologies, the *Mahabarata*, and, God help us, the Bible. I talked about the job of midwifing whatever coherence could be found in occasional pieces and arranging the book to enhance it. A miscellany contained, but wasn't, autobiography. Its creed is: "What I've seen, thought and written about somehow counts."

The second miscellany, *The Invention of the Real* (1982), sported a single prefatory paragraph, whose center was a line from Bunyan's "Apology for His Book": "May not I write in such a style as this?"

This third miscellany assumes here and now that it's part of a tradition. It should need no apology or explanation, but I don't have the confidence to dispense with them. In part, this book reacts to criticism of the first two by the novelist Thomas Rogers. He talked about the absence of self-revelation there. (A friend, he knows what could be revealed.) Rogers quoted an unfortunate sentence: "I've never felt intimate with myself."

That, he said, was the nub of the matter. I'd thought the books top-heavy with "I." Now, though, and not just to please a friend, the "I" is letting down a little more of what hair he has.

The question is "How to do it?" One can work toward memoir, a sort of mnemonic sea in which you hook the fish of your interest. In their memoirs, Yeats and Ford Madox Ford do this with such confident charm that the issue of veracity would be *infra dig.* I adore the results but lack the confidence and gift to aim at them. Yet the stiffer gatherings of Forster (*Abinger Harvest* or *Two Cheers for Democracy*), Lawrence (*Phoenix*) or other "gatherings of fugitives" didn't please me either. The formal model here is Mailer's *Advertisements for Myself.* The intensity and ubiquity of its first person is too much for me, but I like its variety and nonchalant formal devices. (An example of this is the italics which ride on the standard typeface to show that the present tense is partly judging, partly wondering at the old "I's" moves and turns.)

Choosing that form, can one avoid the imputation of self-advertisement? No. One just has to keep doing such things as saying "one" and, elsewhere, hope that the reader will not be oppressed by the skull-cracking bray of the English first-person singular.

This book, like its predecessors, has much to do with the relationship between actuality and its literary expression. It has more to do with history and less with politics than its predecessors. There is, though, a similar mix of interests and genres which collectively tell its small story, that of the author's interests in a certain period.

If it and its siblings had been arranged by a more Joycean mind, different times, seasons, body parts, rhetorical devices and who knows what would be popping up here and there. As it is—or they are—the books do revolve around different persons and places as well as interests. The first book had more to do with Chicago and Nixon, the second with Venice and Carter. The geographical and presidential coordinates of this book are Africa and Reagan. They are not close to the book's center. That center has to do with the position of the book's author as it's determined by his descriptions of certain events, places, persons, scenes, books and speculations about them. Erect-correct or upside-down-and-wrong, the author's stance is formed by the pieces and their relationship to each other. The hope is that not only will a few of them interest and divert the reader but that the whole will suggest something equivalent to the position of the body.

# FACTS, DREAMS, STORIES, LIES

*Reason extinguishes her lamp and we are left in darkness.*
*Only fancy can wander in this darkness and create fictions.*
— *Kant quoted by N. Karamzin,* Letters of a Russian
Traveller, *1789–90.*

*The huge Mississippi of falsehood called history . . .*
— *Matthew Arnold*

*The lack of the fabulous may make my work dull, but I shall*
*be satisfied if it be thought useful by those who wish to know*
*the exact nature of events now past . . .*
— *Thucydides*

*Every separate fantasy contains the fulfillment of a wish, and*
*improves on unsatisfactory reality.*
— *Freud*

# INTRODUCTION

Writing is so peculiar and complex an act—making marks which represent sounds which represent thoughts—you'd think it would always be a promoter of self-consciousness. It isn't. Perhaps it's the difficulty of making good sense or entertainment which diverts the writer from self-consciousness. The act of writing even the most egocentric lines seems to alienate the proclaimed narcissist from his self. Yet Western literature might be called a treasury of self-consciousness, the culture's Collective Self.

In Book 8 of the *Odyssey,* King Alcinous tells Odysseus that the bard Demodocus's song about the heroes of Troy shouldn't make him cry since their "life thread was measured in order to become a poem sung for unborn generations"; Western writers have been worrying the relationship between teller and tale, reality and its literary imitation ever since.

Twentieth-century thinkers have altered the boundaries between subject and object, observer and observation as none before. Recent theoreticians of language and literature have made a canon of those who specialized in the destruction of the old borders. Sometimes they use the cannon of the canonized ones on their texts: philology, myth-analysis, analysis of everyday psychopathology and everyday speech are used to blast old discoveries out of the social, economic, sexual, and historic contexts which kept the discoverers from discovering even more.

The recent thinkers talk more about *story* than their "Elder Fathers" (G. Deleuze). The idea is that we're all defined by and

3

trapped in the tribe's stories. These stories are the "master narratives." They use "master narrative devices" to insure social "legitimization." (See Jean-François Lyotard, *La condition postmoderne*, Paris: Editions de Minuit, 1979.) Every personal story is suspect. Roland Barthes talks of "the bad faith attached to any personal narration." Yet it's also self-censored. Jacques Derrida speaks of "the police" who force "the narratorial voice" to become conscious of "what 'exactly' " it is saying.

The Russian Thaw and the Chinese Great Leap Forward were stopped midstream—or mid-air—by debates over a play and a novel. Perhaps this renewed in Western teachers of language and literature the notion that their critical job was also a revolutionary one. In any event, their *deconstruction* of texts implicates the naive, the hypocritical, and the destructive hierarchies of society.

Deconstruction begins in the refusal to suspend disbelief. To a degree, all critics deconstruct: that is, they conscientiously withdraw enchanted allegiance to the text. Great critics—an Erich Auerbach, a George Orwell, an Edmund Wilson, a Hugh Kenner—have the knack of almost simultaneously suspending and refusing to suspend disbelief. They consume and analyze at the same time. They are the *Guides Michelin* to literature. Anyone who has read or heard anything to which he responds peculiarly because of his own peculiarity has taken the first step toward the deconstruction technique. The fat person who reads about obesity, the black man who reacts to a metaphor about slaves, the Jew who loses aesthetic distance during *The Merchant of Venice*, the Arab-American who remarks the omission* of his ethnic ingredient from a melting-pot recipe, the woman sensitized to the "otherness" of woman who shrivels at the metaphors of male dominance in almost every literary classic, has already deconstructed the text. None of us is liberated from the nar-

---

*Omission, negativity, *Verneinung,* and absence are key terms in recent theoretical discussion as they were for Heidegger, Freud (whose essay on *Verneinung,* "Negation" [vol. 19 of the Standard Edition] is the central text), and such thinkers as Leo Strauss, who, like other "Kabbalistic" thinkers, is waiting to be discovered by French thinkers and their American disciples.

rowness of our being, and so no one is not some sort of deconstructor. On the other hand, culture depends on the suspension of peculiar reaction, the reimmersion in naiveté. All artists who count deconstruct, that is, dissociate from the familiar; however, what makes them count has, I think, little to do with the will to dissociate. They are following the force of their imagination, and it is still a genuine service of criticism to chart that force. This means, taking the writers *at their word.* It means experiencing them naively before making analytic sense of their work.

This section is made up of fairly naive accounts of works which have fascinated me and of some theories of my own. Sometimes the procedure is familiar: one piece I call a "travelogical essay"; another is a two-page reflection on a film. A third is an account of a theory of symbolism followed by a few personal words about the theoretician. Some are fairly thorough, some are fly-by-night or by-the-seat-of-my-pants. Most revolve about the crucial mental distinction between what is felt as truth and what isn't, and between lies aimed at worldly deception and those controlled by the conventions of art. In short, the section has much to do with history and fiction and with matters antecedent to or dependent on them.

# HUNOS AND HISTORIANS, EPIGONES
# AND DREAMERS

*Although I revised the following piece, I did not pry it loose from
its origin. It was given in a series named for the historian Louis
Gottschalk. As a reader can see, Gottschalk is as much a part of
the piece as the places I wrote it are. The reader may not enjoy
the genre—Memorial Essays on the Run—but I do. I think the
model for the travel part of the essay is Thomas Mann's "Sea-
Voyage with* Don Quixote." *Such a piece reminds the writer of
the pleasant circumstances of composition, and his job is to give
the reader some of that pleasure, if only to soften him up for the
argument.*

I'm surprised and proud to be giving the Louis Gottschalk
Memorial Lecture. Surprised, since I'm not only not a historian,
I am—as a small-time fiction writer—the occasional butt of historian friends. They don't but might call me an anti-historian,
or perhaps, a historian of anti-fact. Still, fiction writers often
poach on historical ground, pose as historians and call their
unhistorical works "histories." More concerned with "Once upon
a time" than any particular time, fiction does, however, live in
the past and uses special past—narrative—tenses to show that.
Like the historian's, the fiction writer's sensibility is saturated
with a past he wants to preserve (even when he's ridiculing it).
I believe that Louis Gottschalk, as much as any master of historic
fact and method, understood and appreciated the sorts of distinction I hope to make here. For that reason, and in tribute to

6

him, despite a weariness with lecturing—for I write these words in the midst of an eight-week lecture tour of West, Central, and East Africa—I will do my best to avoid dishonoring that part of my past where Louis lives.

I wasn't an official pupil of his; indeed, we seldom talked about the matters I will talk about here, but certain experiences connected with him are for me at their heart. One has to do with his Memorial Service held in Bond Chapel at the University of Chicago shortly after his death in 1975. That day, many fine things were said about Louis and his life, and they were said in fine ways, but I left the service wondering, "Where's the Louis I knew? Where's the man with the eagle profile and rasping voice, the ironist, the wit? Where's the man who grew out of the boy who never forgot the life in the Brooklyn bar above which his family lived while he immersed himself in eighteenth and early nineteenth-century France? Where is the brilliant historian who came up against the limits of history, feeling the essential inertness in the task he'd set himself, the re-creation of the Marquis de Lafayette's life?" Louis knew the past was always ready to trick those who wanted to salt its tail. A cache of letters could turn up in an attic here, a diary would tumble out of some old bookstore. Perhaps it was this sense of the labyrinthine difficulties of historical reconstruction that led to his sympathy with the pursuits of people like myself. In any case, after that Memorial Service, I felt the sadness not only of Louis's death, but of the oblivion into which uniqueness so often sinks. Not only was a marvelous man gone, it was unlikely that anyone with a tenth of his talent would do for him even a fragment of what he'd done for Lafayette. I thought then and still think how many marvelous and even famous men and women disappear from the earth, leaving little more than the ever-shorter wake of their loved ones' anguish. Of course, work remains, but the uniqueness of personality and appearance, the weight and contradictions of character, these are blotted into the infinity of Non-History. Around that time, I remember suggesting to my colleagues that we start a university portrait gallery. Robert Hutchins, for instance, was still alive. An old friend of his was

7

supposedly engaged in writing a biography, but decades passed and nothing appeared. Hutchins was willing—he told me so—to talk about his life, and his old friends and enemies were still around with plenty of Hutchins stories, but one by one they were going, too. That remarkable men and their remarkable doings were daily turning into what would never be remarked doubled the pain of loss.

As I said, I received the invitation to give this lecture—and am actually writing these words—several thousand miles from Chicago. I'm in West Africa, in the town of Lomé, the capital city of the country of Togo. This morning I spoke to students at the National University here. I went over, line by line, a short story they'd read and saw how much of what had been written far away in Chicago was not only understood but *felt* by these young men and women who'd come from the villages of Togo, Ghana, and Nigeria. I had to explain such things in the story as the game of bridge and a few American customs, but the story's human situation—a very old man seeing his wife of sixty years for the last time—seemed to become part of their lives, and we were briefly united by that imaginary, if realistic event.

Two days earlier the cultural shoe was on the other foot. I'd been driven to the town of Agbodrafo and from there was poled across Lake Togo by a young boatman. We landed at Togoville, the former German capital (from which the country was to take its name). There was the white church built by missionaries with its murals of local martyrs, and in front, the painted pirogue which had brought the statue of Our Lady of Lake Togo to the cathedral. The boatman was a native of the village. He walked us to the pebbled monument which commemorated the treaty which the German diplomat Gustav Nachtigal had signed with King Mlalpa in 1884. Beyond this monument to African concessions were the dirt streets of the village and the conical red cob-and-palm-thatched huts. A tiny goat cried for its mother, and we followed it and the smallest chickens I'd ever seen in and out of dirt streets where barefoot children walked and barefoot women suckled babies and roasted corn. The boatman led us to the town's center, where, under a small pavilion of baked clay, was the village fetish, a parti-colored Picasso-esque sculpture of a woman. There we laid a donation, a hundred Central African francs (forty American cents). The guide took it to the Master of the Fetish, the Huno, the village historian-musician, the official rememberer and inspirer of this village. The Huno was sitting in the shade of an acacia tree with five village elders, three in Western shirts and pants, two, like the Huno himself, bare-torsoed above a mid-section swathed in brilliant orange and black cloth. They greeted us with that marvelous, special charm of West Africa, a kind of inspired tolerance and kindness which one wishes could be bottled and exported instead of ivory and animal skins. The Huno had an idea and transmitted it through our guide. Could we perhaps change some American money he had? Of course. We followed him into his small house, surprisingly cool and pleasant, and while he searched for the money, drank a bit of his home-brewed dynamite. An attentive young boy sat there, the Huno's son, already training to succeed him as Master of the Fetish. The Huno returned, a two-dollar bill in his hand—one of its attractions is, apparently, Thomas Jefferson's portrait—and I gave him the appropriate francs. We exchanged smiles and the mild African handshake and parted forever.

Now why do I spend time on this small incident, one which other tourists can duplicate and with which they have bored friends for decades, if not centuries? I do it, I think, because it strikes me that this amiable Huno belongs with Louis Gottschalk and myself somewhere on the spectrum of those who re-create the past, though in very different ways and for different reasons. A Huno's patrol of the past is heavily mnemonic. For him, the past is severe as the order of beads on a necklace or that of the notes in a musical score. The order of recollection is as crucial as what's recollected. The Huno's history is incantatory, priestly, ritualistic. He is a historian in that he uses the selected detail of a believed past as his material, but his job is less to depict than to inspire, to make his fellows realize who they are and what their ancestors have been. Like Dante's infernal Ulysses, he calls on his tribe to "*Considerate la vostra semenza.*" "Consider your seed. You were made not to live like brutes, but to follow virtue and conscience." If he varies his recital, it can only be—as I understand it—to fit new matter into the rigid categories of the old. He is a kind of human transmission molecule, and part of his job is to replicate himself. His son stands by, learning the old tales in the old way, and will differ as little from his father as his father from his. I assume that under the stress of social catastrophe or even individual power, a mutation is possible here as it is in the case of the chemical molecule; but if the mutation is too violent, transmission will not occur. On the other hand, my guess is that a Huno can introduce small variations into the ceremonial recital and survive as an admirable practitioner of his calling.

What about the man *we* call historian? His job is a complicated one. As Fernand Braudel puts it in one of the prefaces to his famous work on the Mediterranean, it is the simultaneous depiction of "both that conspicuous history which holds our attention by its continual and dramatic changes—and that other, submerged, history, almost silent and always discreet, virtually unsuspected either by its observers or its participants."* To some degree, especially in these archaeological-anthropological centuries, that double task involves the excavation and appraisal of every sort of evidence, geographic, geologic, demographic, botanic, epistolary, artistic, whatever. But the question remains, "Evidence of *what*, records of *what*?" Erasmus hated the portrait Albrecht Dürer made of him and wrote, "If you don't understand what a tree is, you won't be able to draw a leaf." The historian's *what* is crucial. For Braudel, it was a world defined by a certain quantity of $H_2O$, the Mediterranean. For Louis Gottschalk, it was a human being, Lafayette. For Donald Lach, it is the influence of one large part of the world, Asia, on the transformation of another, Europe. The choice of a *what* is crucial.

---

*Preface to the Second Edition (June 19, 1963), *The Mediterranean and the Mediterranean World in the Age of Philip II*, trans. Sian Reynolds (New York: Harper and Row, 1972), I, 16.

"It is," Einstein told Heisenberg in a talk that changed the young man's life, "Theory which determines what we observe." What historian working after Ranke would dare to bend such an axiom? Fiction writers are accustomed to it. They deal with it technically under the rubric "point of view," but, as Braudel points out, "the historian hasn't the novelist's freedom." He cannot control his subject this way.* It goes against the grain of actuality as defined by the famous Rankean expression, *"Wie es eigentlich gewesen ist." As it really was.***

Yet one must somehow assume a tree among the data of bark, leaf, branch, and rootage. One must assume a finitude of data. Louis Gottschalk knew that the 365 days of his years could never reassemble the 365-day years of the Marquis de Lafayette, and, like all historians, was forced to devise all sorts of *whats* to handle Lafayette's life. He supplied sections, patterns, theories, points of view, a hundred tentative *whats* which permitted the continuity of his research. Not that he threw in the towel of assembling the data. In seminars, every student would be assigned a day in the hero's life. (This was an industrialist's approach to the problem of data production.) Even every day is infinitely complex and can never be reproduced *wie es eigentlich gewesen ist.* The point was to find principles of inclusion undeformed by ideology or even idea, by weakness or bias. If I read Louis correctly, his principles, like Braudel's, were grounded in his own sense of human experience, controlled by his belief that—as he wrote—the historian's "imagination is directed toward re-creation, not creation."† Submitted to peers, tested by the canons of historical evidence and writing, by hu-

*Ibid., I, 17.

**I wondered why the superfluity of the *"eigentlich,"* that "really," hadn't been remarked until I understood that the expression should be translated "as it was experienced at the time." Otherwise, one fifth of this famous characterization would be emphatic, an imposed tone which almost subverts its intention.

†"The Historian and the Historical Document," in *The Use of Personal Document in History, Anthropology and Sociology* by Louis Gottschalk, Clyde Kluckhohn, and Robert Angell, *Social Science Research Council Bulletin* 53 (1945): 9.

man reason and imagination, the emergent history would be the finest depiction of both the "conspicuous" and "submerged" past that a historian could make. The verbal re-creation of the flesh, movement, pressures, forces, relationships, character, governance and inspiration of the past would be there, filtered only by the trained honesty of a particular temperament. The tempering of that temperament would not result in the magnification of bias, but in its diminution.

It's here that the historian—whether narrator or Braudelian annalist—differs from even the most reportorial, most mimetic, and most naturalistic novelist. Few fiction writers of these last centuries would deny that their own temperament is an essential ingredient of their work. Observations, feelings and sensations, sense of form, symmetry, diction, scene and action, brand of sadness and humor, these constitute the inflection, tonality, rhythm, and ultimate character of fictional evocation whether the subject of the fiction be more or less remembered, more or less *made up*.

If the historian's re-creation of the past more and more resembles its original, the fiction writer's grows more and more different from its. In fictionalized actuality, temperament and art arbitrate every detail. If the chief desire is to commemorate a past, love and hatred will eventually dominate and transfigure it. And yet, this loving-hating image-dominated fiction writer's summoning of lost time and people, bent along the lines of temperament, art, and bias, often evokes a past realer than any other, one with the primal power evoked by those sudden bursts of feeling full of taste and odor which return to us epiphanically what we once knew and once were. Why it should be that the arbitrary impositions and deformations of art should be able to resuscitate the past in this way is as mysterious as the symmetry which astrophysicists make out of the infinities of the universe. The resuscitation, often begun as commemoration, celebration, or denunciation, ends with the formation of something totally new, yet that novelty carries a kind of force which seems as lifelike as life. No Huno can match such creation. It may be the very artifice, the very suspension of normal attention, which surprises us with the power of illusion. The narrative manipulation of attention—the shifts from external description to internal monologue, from present tense to past, from event to sensuous description and from that to dialogue and argument—somehow creates a pattern which resembles that of feeling itself, that feeling which is the mode of human experience beneath and beyond intellect. Whatever the case, the art conjured out of feeling both mimics and expresses it. So it "creates" the world which becomes our sense of the past. *Bleak House is* nineteenth-century London, *Madame Bovary is* provincial Normandy, *Ulysses is,* in this strange way, more Dublin than Dublin's buildings, streets, and citizens. As for the precisely named *A la recherche du temps perdu* by that most brilliantly temperamental of all literary artists, Marcel Proust, it is not only a great part of early twentieth-century France, it is the *process* of its evocation.

I write this last paragraph sitting by a window overlooking the emerald palms of a coconut grove along the southwest shore of the town of Libreville, the beautiful equatorial capital city of the country of Gabon. I've just finished writing in my journal an account of a jeep ride to a tiny village a few kilometers away from the glass-and-white-stone town. This was a filthy cluster of tin-and-board-roofed huts where one or two hundred people whose original home is the distant forest village of M'bigou work the famous stone of that village into the solemn heads and animals, ashtrays and vases which, fired and stained by *Johnson's Wax,* are sold here in town as Gabon's best-known artifacts. There are very few smiles on the faces of the men who chip away at the stone or on the women giving suck or cooking at the fires. Roosters and geckos—the marvelous orange-headed lizards who seem to be doing push-ups or genuflecting when they aren't chasing each other—a few scrawny goats and a dog or two move around with sad children who squat here and there doing nothing. The floors of the houses are dirt, the furniture is sparse and ugly, and the only decorations I saw were a few old photographs fixed to doorway struts. The carved heads and animals are beautiful but monotonous. One does not have the sense that this is a village of proud artisans, let alone fine artists. It does not resemble those villages in Bali where the urge to beautify reaches everything, so that every pillar is sculpted and every other movement has a balletic quality. There the art and celebration fuse as a way of making and living. This outpost of exiled M'bigouans has more the quality of a small factory where the workers have been subdued into equivalents of machine-parts. Here they reproduce the inventions of the past with mechanical skills. They do not employ the energy of individual reenactment that the Huno of Togoville employed. They certainly lack the mastery, dedication, and interpretive brilliance of the fine historian. And they are furthest of all from that tenacious dream-extended transfiguration of the literary artist. Yet it occurs to me now that these melancholy stone chippers could be mistaken by careless examination for any one of the others. They imitate old patterns, their object is not innovation but re-creation of what was, and the results of their work seem at first glance to have the beauty of spontaneity. My point here is that in each category of human production and fruition, there are epigones, imitators and *stakhanovites*, who may be passed off as the real thing.

In this coursing discourse, this essay on the African run, the next stop is in Kenya. I write from a beautiful lodge set amidst the enormous game preserve of the Masai Mara near the Tanzania border, adjacent to the Serengeti Plain. For two days we've been chasing elephant, giraffe, Thompson and Grant gazelle, buffalo, baboons, wildebeest and zebra—those *lumpenproletariat* of this animal world—warthogs, impala, you name it. This morning, instead of going out in a car, we waited on a lawn while a crew operated blowers and gas heaters to raise an immense cloth pancake into a magnificent nine-story-high orange and golden bulb, beautiful as some Southern dream of Christmas. Five of us followed the New Zealand pilot into a small wicker basket—made, I nervously noted, by members of the Royal Society for the Blind. The basket—very well made it was—was held by guy lines to the balloon. With release and a burst of flame fueled by the methane cylinders, up we rose in the air toward, through, and above the clouds, and, taking the wind, drifted over the amazing fields, the thorn and acacia trees, the long green miles empty of all but the beautiful animals. Occasional elephant and giraffe looked up at the astonishing ascension with the barest surprise. Up and down we rode, sometimes scarcely a yard from treetops or the ground itself, silently following the wild beauties. Then, just where the Sand River widens before the Tanzania border, a hundred miles or so from the gorge where the Leakeys decided that men became themselves, down we came. Magically, a crew which had followed us in a truck grounded the balloon, extracted us and then the gas cylinders. These they laid on the ground, put mats between them, and, on the mats, laid baskets of chicken, cheese, and croissants and iced buckets of champagne.

So here it was, this expensively realized dream of international elegance, Eden made real and brilliantly commercial, courtesy of the Block family, the great hotel keepers of Kenya.

The night before, nervous about getting up at six to be ready for the flight, I woke from a real dream, one intricate as a novel of intrigue, so vivid that I felt all I needed to do was write down what I'd dreamt. It was full of Nazi impersonators, substituting for real Nazis who had been chilled in aspic or stuffed with chocolate and laid out on a beautiful buffet. Meanwhile, my wife dreamed of a wave that was Metaphor, a wave which dashed humans into letters of the alphabet and then reassembled them.

I describe these dreams, one the actualized semi-absurdity of luxury amidst the wilds of Masai land, the others, the nocturnal manufacture of human mental apparatus, in order to contrast the spectrum of preservation about which I've talked with things that are also, in their way, preservations of the past, either as fragments of antiquated notions of human elegance or as the recycled oneiric garbage of old fears and wishes. Where do these dreams fit into our account of re-creators and preservers?

The dream of champagne amidst the world of beasts is, in its way, the ultimate expression of a materialist culture, a kind of sensuous equivalent of the fetishes and panaceas, the rituals and

15

graded privileges of the Huno's village. It gives a selected few the sense that they are kings of the earth, and offers the rest a dream of aspiration, a payoff for their daily sweat. It supplies this in the form of that artificial simplicity which Marie Antoinette experienced as she dressed as a milkmaid to play with her ladies around the *hameau*. For a historian, this luxury may represent the conspicuous display of such imitation and may be part of a historical theory which examines surplus capital and the exploitation of labor. For the fiction writer, this luxuriant dream depends, like all else he describes, on the use made of it in the larger context of his fiction. It would be one kind of event in Agatha Christie, another in Alain Robbe-Grillet. For a writer like me, the things that count would be the color, the air, the diction (the variety of flora and fauna names, the mix of Kiswahili, English, Kimasai, and Gikiyu), the narrative possibilities of such a balloon flight with its invitation to stray over closed borders perhaps to the Olduvai Gorge for the kind of contrast Scott Fitzgerald obtained at the beginning of *The Last Tycoon*, where the ruined film magnate finds himself at Andrew Jackson's Hermitage in Nashville. The point is that such a happening could be crucial to my work, whereas it could only be incidental to the historian or the Huno unless, say, some significant personage had died in the course of this luxurious indulgence or if it crucially signified an area's disposition of resources.

The nocturnal dreams could also be parts of fictional narratives and could even play roles in historical ones, if, say, they were the accurately reported dreams of a Lincoln or a Caesar before their assassinations. But there is something more important which differentiates this particular fragment of experience for the fiction writer. Dreams come from a level of conception which is close to the one which generates the emotional power of his work. For such writers as Graham Greene, dreams are a source of fictional subjects and actions. For Franz Kafka, the dream form, its peculiar logic linking what could not be linked in actuality, becomes the form of the fiction. For a realistic writer, such as myself, the dream is an expansion of the temperament which I've come to trust as the source of what often counts most in my work. The Huno and the historian must work for generalization and significance. What ultimately counts for them is understanding, explanation, or ritual binding. Individual experience must not overflow understanding or ritual. For the fiction writer, the power which has generated the dream is at least a cousin of the one which his art attempts to frame, and it may be that his trust in it is what makes his evocation of the past, deformed as it is by art and temperament, the powerful actuality it can be.

I write the final section of this "travelogical" essay back home in Chicago. Some of the accumulated mail is answered, a bill or two has been paid, students' papers are being read, recommendations written, and I've managed to teach a few classes. My bags are unpacked, the papers, postcards, and souvenirs are getting sorted out.

My mental baggage will not be unpacked for some time. Eight weeks of novel experience will take anyone, let alone a novelist, quite some time to sort out.

The last few days of the trip were saturated by something which made me know it belonged in this lecture. It began at five-thirty A.M. the last Tuesday in March. We were sitting in a waiting room at Cairo Airport in that state of barely animated suspension which hits travelers, especially after they have passed through the indignities of what are called "formalities," customs, passport and baggage checks. Here we were, a group of heterogenous people of ten or so nationalities held together by little more than a wait for a flight to Rome. A man across from me said something to a young couple on his right. I thought I heard the word "President" and something else that hinted at sickness or death. It occurred to me that President Begin of Israel was dead, he'd had heart attacks, and this would be something that would be heard about quickly in Egypt. It couldn't have been President Sadat, that would have caused too much excitement here. Then another word made me know it was someone else. I asked the gentleman, an Egyptian, who said he'd heard on the early morning news that President Reagan had been shot. Devastating. No political supporter I, but that had no bearing on my feelings. I felt eviscerated. What had happened? Within a minute, this man's news supply was exhausted: a young white man had shot Reagan; he was still alive; others were shot, one at least killed. I asked an Egyptian Air Lines stewardess if she knew more. She'd heard a later broadcast and gave a few more details. Within minutes, the group of travelers was galvanized by the need to hear the story and to make sense of it. We passed each other information, and when the *Egyptian Gazette* appeared, we passed it around and read the confirmation of the accuracies and inaccuracies we'd heard. Within an hour, we'd accommodated ourselves to the shock, and en route to our first stop in Athens, most of us were able to read other things and to eat our breakfast with the special relish of air travelers. Over the Mediterranean, the TWA pilot made an announcement that the president had been operated on and was now recovering, his condition was stable, the prognosis excellent. Relief, and then, boredom. Two hours later, en route to the *Stazione Termini* in Rome, an American who'd been in Boston the day before gave us more detail. No one was killed, the villain was a twenty-five-year-old blond fellow, son of a "rich oil man," name of Hinckley. In Rome, the wonderful Italian newspapers were full of details and pictures. Over cappuccino and my beloved *giambelli*—marvelous light doughnuts I buy near Largo Argentina—I read the accounts of Hinckley's history, his gun purchases, his arrest in Nashville, his trip to Dallas.

In my head patterns were forming: the actor President shot by another man acting in the American tradition of the lone gunman-cowboy. Now though, the actor was victim instead of assassin (à la John Wilkes Booth). This was a new twist in the American story. My own pattern included the royal tombs, the *mastabas* and pyramids, I'd been visiting. How many assassinations had those geometric dreams of the desert witnessed? And here in Rome, itself full of Egyptian imitations, hieroglyphs and obelisks within steps of my own hotel, so many more stories, though of the Roman conspiratorial pattern. Each day brought more detail and demanded deeper patterns. It turned out the act

# CHICAGO AS FICTION

There is an enormous, magisterial, and almost never read doctoral dissertation in the stacks of the University of Chicago's Regenstein Library. Its author is the late Lennox Grey, the title— not one of the century's catchiest—*Chicago and the "Great American Novel": A Critical Approach to the American Epic.* It is a survey, classification, and analysis of the approximately five hundred novels by two hundred different authors set in Chicago up to 1935. The novels are classified by period and subject. There are groups about Chicago as a Portage, a Fort, a Trading Post, a Boomtown, an Agricultural Metropolis before and after the Civil War and the Great Fire of 1871, Chicago the Industrial City, the White City, the Black, and the Modern City.

Nothing comparable has been written since, though Chicago is at least as complex a place as it was before 1935 and those who have set novels here are every bit as serious and able as their predecessors. Such surveys as Michael Anania's "A Commitment to Grit" (*Chicago,* Nov. 1983, 200–207) may be excellent in their way, but such a subject needs the leisurely immensity of a dissertation and the heroic patience of a Lennox Grey.

Grey's thesis is that Chicago has been regarded as the most American of American cities and, therefore, the most appropriate setting for that literary unicorn, "the Great American Novel." Its geographic centrality, its rapid transformations, the exceptional individuals—especially transgressors and over-

21

reachers—and the myths which local and national media excogitated from them, its tradition of being untraditional, its ethnic variety, its inventive, clamorous commerce and industry, its old status as junction and port, and, finally, its tradition of literary vaunting and self-explanation, make it the ideal "writer's town."

Whether or not it is more of a writer's town than New Orleans or Bordeaux, Worcester, Massachusetts or Worcester, Worcestershire, is itself a complicated question. If, say, a group of Brontë-like sisters grew up in Worcester, Mass., it might become more a writer's town than, say, Moline, Illinois or even Kansas City, Missouri. Yet it is a fact that so many writers seem to have had something to do with Chicago that sixty-seven years ago H. L. Mencken was able to call it the "Literary Capital of the United States." Mencken's extravagance was widely circulated and probably stimulated what it described. "In Chicago," he wrote,

> there is a mysterious something that makes for individuality, personality, charm. . . . Find a writer who is indubitably American in every pulse beat . . . and in nine times out of ten you will find he has some sort of connection with the Gargantuan abbatoir by Lake Michigan.

This sort of rhapsody with its "mysterious something" and its "American in every pulse beat" is easy to grasp by unthinking and unliterary people, but on page after literary page, as Grey shows, it represents the note struck about this city: Chicago is the *real* America, the place where individuality—America's very juice—runs clearest. Fourteen years before Mencken's hyperbole, William Dean Howells, writing in the *North American Review,* spelled out the Chicago connection to the Declaration of Independence.

> The republic of letters is elsewhere sufficiently republican, but in the metropolis of the Middle-West, it is so almost without thinking, almost without feeling; and the atmospheric democracy, the ambient equality, is something that runs like the prime effect in literature of what America has been doing and saying in life ever since she first formulated herself in the Declaration.

Facts, Dreams, Stories, Lies

This is less hyperbolical, but who can get away with such personifications today? Howells's remarks make a Chicagoan suspicious. "Ambient equality"? "Atmospheric democracy"? Who the hell is he kidding? What's he selling? America either says nothing or so much that you can't summarize it, especially with polysyllabic phrases, yet Chicago is as much a verbal as a stone and metal construction. Its verbal versions are as distinct, as salable, and as potent as the products it puts into boxes or electronic blips. Free-associate with "Chicago" and you get something very different than "Los Angeles." Los Angeles conjures up Disney miniatures, Hollywood illusions, Watts Tower's junk beauty, San Simeon pretense. It's Polynesia on wheels, a rainbow fragility menaced by grinding tectonic plates, fires, smog, the automobile freeway. With Chicago, the word "real" comes to mind. Farce amid grimness. Fires and fists, strikes, riots, clubs and cops, machine tools and machine politics, crooks and cardinals (sometimes fused, as in Andrew Greeley's fiction or in Nicholas V. Hoffman's recent novel, *Organized Crimes* [Harper and Row, 1985]).

Chicago belongs on the drama as well as the front page. The personae include the Boss, the Corrupt Alderman with heart and pockets of gold, the Deal-Maker, the Speechifying Smoothie, the Rhetorician, Municipal Sheep, The Syndicate, His Eminence—whose treasure is not exclusively celestial. America is entranced by Chicago characters. It expects, wants and needs this literary fix of fraud, con, toughness and slaughter. It's Disneyland—no, it's Oberammergau with real nails and real blood.

Since Chicago grew as popular journalism did, it was early legendary. The east needed explanations of this noisy child of the lake. Chicago's writers slaked this eastern appetite. In the columns of Ade, Dunne, Lardner, Hecht, Royko, Greene, Roger Simon, and twenty others, the Chicago comedy was the stuff of daily yuks. The columns' heroes are the abused and the abusive, the poor slobs and the Paddies, Mikes, Vitos, Big Als, Fast Eddies, and Crazy Janes who run them into the ground.

The novelists, at least the ones who will be read next year as well as this, lie in back of the newspaper characters and con-

23

ceptions. Even when their books are based on historical characters and events, it is the coherence of their imaginative world which survives. Dreiser's financial genius, Cowperwood, is based on the traction tycoon Yerkes, but he is more Dreiser than Yerkes. Dreiser's heroes come to Chicago in a trance. They turn the city into a field to be plowed, a pocket to be picked, a stage to be filled. They want everything. Money isn't enough, power isn't enough. What they ultimately want is explanation. "If he had not been a great financier," writes Dreiser of Cowperwood,

> and above all, a marvelous organizer, he might've become a highly individualistic philosopher. . . . His business, as he saw it, was with the material facts of life, or rather, with those third and fourth degree theorems and syllogisms which control material things and so represent wealth.

2

Material. Stuff. The real. The mass and variety of urban matter requires ever subtler shorthand to register and manipulate it.* The enchantment and the curse of matter have been the great Chicago theme.

> Chicago is an instance of a successful, contemptuous disregard of nature by man. . . . In . . . Chicago, man has decided to make for himself a city for his artificial necessities in defiance of every indifference displayed by nature. Along the level floor of sand and gravel cast up by the mighty lake, the city has swelled and pushed, like a pool of quicksilver, which, poured out on a flat plate, is ever undulating and alternating its borders as it eats its way further into the desert expanse. Railroad lines, like strands of a huge spider's web, run across the continent in all directions, wilfully, strenuously centering in this waste spot, the swampy corner of a great lake.**

*The Chicago futures market would have excited medieval philosophers.
**Robert Herrick, *The Gospel of Freedom.*

24

The threat is quasi-Marxist: what's hauled in, the material of wealth, threatens to "become you."* In novels, Chicago is the emblem of mastered nature, and it pays for its mastery. Mrs. O'Leary's cow was the revenge of the prairie. Even in the Chicago sections of non-Chicago novels you hear the dirge of wealth. Scott Fitzgerald's most destructive characters come from Chicago. In *Tender Is The Night,* the Swiss psychiatrist in charge of Nicole, the broken Chicago heiress, tells Dick Diver he's often treated the victims of these rich Chicagoans. Nicole's father, the millionaire meat-packer, is, like Cowperwood, a transgressor, but the boundary he's crossed is kinship. Incest with Nicole has driven her mad. After years of treatment, the cured Nicole becomes herself a ruinous transgressor. Her beauty, intelligence, and wealth ruin the husband who saved her. But there are more remote victims.

> Nicole bought from a great list that ran two pages and bought the things in the window besides. Everything she liked that she couldn't possibly use herself, she bought as a present for a friend. She bought colored beads, folding beach cushions, artificial flowers, honey, a guest bed, bags, scarves, love birds, miniatures for a doll's house and three yards of a new cloth the color of prawns. She bought a dozen bathing suits, a rubber alligator, a traveling chess set of gold and ivory, big linen handkerchiefs for Abe, two dozen leather jackets of kingfisher blue and burning bush from Hermès—bought all these things not a bit like a highclass courtesan buying underwear and jewels which were after all professional equipment and insurance—but with an entirely different point of view. Nicole was the product of much ingenuity and toil. For her sake trains began their run at Chicago and traversed the round belly of the continent to California; chicle factories burned and link belts grew link by link in factories; men mixed toothpaste in vats and drew mouthwash out of copper hogsheads; girls canned tomatoes quickly or worked rudely at the Five-and-Ten on Christmas Eve; half-breed Indians toiled on Brazilian coffee plantations and dreamers were muscled out of patent rights in new tractors—these

*Edgar Lee Masters, *Children in the Marketplace.*

were some of the people who gave a tithe to Nicole, and as the whole system surged and thundered onward, it lent a feverish bloom to such processes of hers as wholesale buying . . .

In our time, the extravagance of the rich (see the birthday party for the Great Dane in Bellow's *The Dean's December*) is comedy, not indictment.

In the thirties, forties and fifties, the Chicago writers James Farrell and Nelson Algren spent no time on the rich; they described the—usually—defeated poor. Farrell—one of the few Chicago writers actually born in the city—tracks the degradation of poor Irish Catholics. His description of their communities makes Joyce's exhausted Dublin look like Pericles' Athens. Farrell's Chicagoans are ignorant, bored, mindless and violent. Only now and then does a whiff of poetry stir one of them. A lake breeze, a kiss, a fight raises them from their piggish life, but there's no hope it will change things. Only at the end, regret and nostalgia touch them with something more. But their poetry is shallow; the nostalgia is Verlaine's "garlic of low cuisine."

For Algren, Chicago is the beauty with the busted nose. It's Sancho Panza-Charlie Chaplin Chicago, that of tough little guys making music out of abuse and loss. The Algren characters just want small stakes, just want to make it through the day, but the day is controlled by the Big Shots and those who work for them. They leave the Algren loser nothing but booze, dope, and the bodies of other losers. Fine with him; he hates winners.

Ten or fifteen years before his death, Algren sensed that his Chicago poetry had run out. He more or less left the city to a writer who found poetry in its winners and its losers, in be-Sulkaed Loop finaglers and old Jews taking steam with smalltime hoods in Division Street bathhouses, even in professors and deans.* Bellow's heroes are also acquisitive border-crossers, but

*Like many Chicago writers of the last ninety years, Saul Bellow has been associated with the University of Chicago, but unlike many of those writers—Philip Roth, Austin Wright, Thomas Rogers, Robert Coover, James Purdy, Kurt Vonnegut, Douglas Unger, Janet Kauffman, and many others—he wasn't a transient for whom a few years of school-time were an icon of carnival or Paradise.

26

their borders are sensuous, intellectual, and spiritual. Bellow's books are education novels, and his heroes are educated by great men and great books as well as by the thugs, lawyers, businessmen, con men, and splendid ladies of the city. The Bellow hero is heavy with memory. The Chicago of the twenties presses on the Chicago of the sixties, seventies, and eighties. (There are geniuses of memory as well as geniuses of fact and theory.) No writer has written longer or better about this city than Bellow, and, of course, as he has changed, so have his versions of it. In early Bellow, people work in coalyards, haberdasheries, Loop department stores, lake resorts. Wherever they work, they classify, analyze, transform fact into theory, theory into poetry. One hero delivers relief checks in the ghetto.

> He had four or five blocks to go, past open lots, old foundations, closed schools, black churches, mounds, and he reflected there must be many people alive who had once seen the neighborhood rebuilt and new. Now there was a second layer of ruins; centuries of history accomplished through human massing. Numbers had given the place forced growth; enormous numbers had also broken it down . . . . Rome, that was almost permanent, did not give rise to thoughts like these . . . . But in Chicago, where the cycles were so fast and the familiar died out, and again rose, changed, and died again in thirty years, you saw the common agreement or covenant, and you were forced to think about appearances and realities.
>
> ("Looking for Mr. Green")

In the latest Bellow stories, meanings aren't conclusions. Memory creates an understanding which transcends meaning. It's as if material Chicago turns out to be its own explanation. Woody Selbst remembers when he worked at the 1933 Century of Progress World's Fair pulling a rickshaw,

> wearing a peaked straw hat and trotting with powerful thick legs, while the brawny, redfaced farmers—his boozing passengers— were laughing their heads off and pestered him for whores, he although a freshman at the seminary, saw nothing wrong when girls asked him to steer a little business their way, in making dates, and accepting tips from both sides. He necked in Grant

# The Position of the Body

Park with a powerful girl who had to go home quickly to nurse her baby. Smelling of milk, she rode beside him on the streetcar to the West Side, squeezing his rickshaw puller's thigh and wetting her blouse. This was the Roosevelt Road car. Then, in the apartment, where she lived with her mother, he couldn't remember that there were any husbands around. What he did remember was the strong milk odor. Without inconsistency, next morning he did Old Testament Greek: the light shineth in the darkness—to fos en te skotia fainei*—and the darkness comprehendeth it not.

("A Silver Dish")

Bellow's Chicago is not the last, only—till now—the most vivid picture of the city, the equivalent of Dickens's London, Joyce's Dublin, the Paris of Stendhal, Balzac, Zola, and Proust.

3

In 1984, *TriQuarterly* published its now—as these things go—famous *Chicago* issue. In it one finds fifteen or twenty new versions of the city. Leon Forrest, Cyrus Colter, Harry Mark Petrakis, Stuart Dybek, Eugene Wildman, and Larry Heinemann are a few of the authors whose transfigured memories or imaginative conjurings of streets, stones, ghettos, trains, of ethnic obtuseness, poetry and chauvinism, of street action and lacustrine musing create what readers will know as Chicago. James Hurt (writing in the best of the city's free newspapers, *The Reader*) said that the issue contains new "alternatives to the Hog Butcher Line" of Chicago writing. "There is a kind of compromised laughter, a survivor's cynicism" but also "sweetness and the awareness of human possibility" in these new Chicagos. He cites Dave Etter's "rejection" of Sandburg's "Chicago":

City of the bent shoulders, the bum ticker, the bad back. City of the called third strike, the blocked punt. City of the ever-deferred dream. City of the shattered windshield, the loose wheel,

*Actually New Testament Greek (John 1).

28

the empty gas tank. City of I remember when, of once upon a time. City not of "I will" but of "I wish I could."

From outsiders as well, the Chicago visions pour. So Nathan Zuckerman returns to Chicago in Philip Roth's *The Anatomy Lesson* and sees its "broken bands of illumination, starred, squared, braided, climbing lights" as a paradisal constellation, while Denis Johnson—in his marvelous first novel *Angels*—transcribes a Chicago nightmare:

> Five billion weirdos walking this way and that, not looking at each other, and every third one had something for sale. Money-lickers; and black pimps dressed entirely in black, and a forest of red high heels. There were lots of lights—everyone had half a dozen shadows scurrying in different directions underneath them.

New tunes in the classic keys. The con, the sell, the paradise of man's energy, Chicago, the setting for excess, rapidity, confusion, gorgeousness, bitter triumph, overreaching, bitter collapse. Since stories attract stories and fictions generate counter-fictions, this most fictionalized of American cities grows ever thicker with its selves, so much so that between the fictions and the actualities, there is hardly room for a shadow.

# ON MRS. LANGER'S *MIND*

Forty years ago, Susanne Langer published *Philosophy in a New Key,* a "theory of mind" which clarified conceptions of symbolism, language, myth, art, and the sacred as the great philosopher-scientists of the century had clarified conceptions of simultaneity, energy, mass, and force. The "new key" had been forged by Russell, Wittgenstein, Freud, Cassirer, and—Mrs. Langer's teacher—Whitehead to "launch the attack on the formidable problem of symbol and meaning." A prime chapter of her book examined the significance of music. Ten years later, Mrs. Langer published *Feeling and Form.* This book expanded the insights into music and applied them to all the arts. In addition to using the key of symbolism—"a symbol is any device whereby we are enabled to make an abstraction"—Mrs. Langer devised—or borrowed—such key notions as "semblance" and "virtual memory" (the mode of narrative) which have since been used by serious thinkers (many of them artists) to talk about the powers of dance and drama, poetry and painting. One notion, that of "living form"—which transforms "felt activity" to "perceptible quality"—"engendered the whole study of mind" which occupied Mrs. Langer since then.

*Mind, III* completed our culture's most coherent examination of nature's living forms. To clarify such concepts as evolution,

Susanne K. Langer, *Mind: An Essay on Human Feeling,* Vol. III. Baltimore: Johns Hopkins University Press, 1984.

instinct, acts, feeling, and mind, Mrs. Langer mastered the technical literature of fifty specialties. (Biologists have told me they know no comparable performance.) Using brilliant research while lopping off the excess interpretations of the researchers, clarifying data in, say, cytology with a concept picked up, say, from linguistics, Mrs. Langer severed such antique conundrums as the relation between mind and body, sensibility and mentation, the inner life of humans and animals. Out went picturesque notions about the "ritual" behavior of fighting wolves, the "courtship" of birds, the "architectural powers" of bower birds, the "communication" of kangaroo rats (for whom sounds are not a form of telephony but of "behavioral reinforcement," the kind of "self-expansion" often seen in animals in whom the organs of hearing and sound production are close together). Volume II discussed the specialization of the hominid stock— posture, skull structure, development of hand as sense organ, cortical availability, the development of that image-and-dream-burdened forebrain which was forced into the abstract resolution of excited impulses. Out of the festal energy of the gregarious hominids came that discrimination of the rumbled chant whose segments, associated with some event, sight or apparition, became the first acts of speech. From speech came the creation of the world of time, the conception of past and future. The final paragraph of Volume II looked ahead to a volume on society, which "like the spatiotemporal world itself is a creation of man's specialised modes of feeling-perception, imagination, conceptual thought and the understanding of language. This membership in a continuous, recognised society . . . epitomises the great shift from beast to man."

Volume III begins with an examination of primitive mentality. It challenges the interpretation of Malinowski about the double system of magical and scientific thought, offering instead Essertier's fifty-year-old idea about *assertion* as an affirmation of mentality equivalent to the child's joy in its own strength as it squeezes an object. It is this self-expansion which helps explain the "irresponsible thinking" of the mythic mentality about a reality which for us, children of mental combat, fiction and

31

science, must be certified by "objective perception" or "trust-worthy information."

Ritual, myth, the discovery of past, future and death, religion, tragedy, the invention of gods, God and the Self, the tension between the surging power of individuality and the society which reminds it of its obligatory membership by significantly maiming it (in, say, circumcision), the building of temples and cities— Near Eastern ones which celebrated royal individuals and thus had to be razed to the ground and those European cities of commerce and convenience which have survived every sort of devastation—the waging of war, the making of empires (including the Inca empires which perished of intellectual stasis).

The book ends, as a great life does, on a note of tragedy. At eighty-eight, Mrs. Langer—who died in 1985—had "to curtail the work at what should be its height," the discussion of epistemology and metaphysics, due to "the hindrances of age— especially increasing blindness." She offered a few brilliant pages on the growth of counting ("the discernment of equally spaced units") out of the pedal symmetry of locomotion, its elaboration in dance and its enhancement by hand-drumming. There are a few paragraphs on the relationship of fact to language and a final, Pisgah sight of the world which the volcanic force of physical science is in the process of creating.

Reviewing Volume II in 1973, I wrote perhaps a bit over-enthusiastically, "If the concluding volume of *Mind* is as brilliant and beautiful as the first two, we shall have seen the philosophical equivalent of that other masterpiece of an octogenarian, the second Deposition of Michelangelo."

Recently, I looked at that marvelous work. Its eighty-nine-year-old sculptor had chipped away at it days before his death. There was the extra arm he'd not yet cut away, there was the still uncarved fusion of the dead Christ and the old Joseph (Michelangelo's self-portrait). But the great conception of the masterpiece was not blurred. There was the magnificence of human conclusion, the beauty of exhausted hope. I do not think it out of place to pair it with this great, sustained production of Susanne Langer, a production whose incompleteness will not, I think, bar it from being joined with the conceptual masterworks of those peers who were her teachers and forerunners.


### AFTERWORD

I knew Mrs. Langer only one year, the year I taught at Connecticut College. This was in 1954–55. She'd just come as chairman of the Philosophy Department. I was an instructor (making, incidentally, $3500 a year). I had read *Philosophy in a New Key* and *Feeling and Form,* her wonderful work on aesthetics. The woman was as remarkable as the books. She was small, lithe, supple. Her eyes were brilliant, her wide mouth slightly bucked. She had an exceptionally alert and innocent face. There was a purity about Mrs. Langer I've encountered only rarely. It was not that she didn't know about the world's harshness. I'm sure she'd known plenty of it. (She'd been divorced.) It was just that her attention was elsewhere. That year she was beginning to collect material for *Mind: An Essay on Human Feeling.* Her powers of concentration were a matter for jokes. Spotting a frog she wished to examine, Mrs. Langer left her car. The car was parked on a railroad track. Inside it was her precious cello. The train totalled both. Mrs. Langer adored music, and to watch her listen to it was itself a kind of music. She appeared to be suffering, yet there were no contortions on her face, just the tension of profound audition. At such moments she was beautiful. A couple of times my wife and I went to her lovely eighteenth-century house in Old Lyme. She had no stove and cooked on a grill over the fire. I didn't feel that she'd dropped out of this century. I felt she was a part of a tradition of permanent contemporaries. Aristotle, Albertus Magnus, Kant, and Hume could have dropped by the house in Old Lyme and felt less out of place than almost anywhere in Connecticut.

# ON TOYNBEE'S *HISTORY*

*One of the great intellectual events of my life was reading the first eight volumes of Toynbee's* A Study of History. *It was a wonderful world tour except that one toured not space but time, intellect, and culture. For an ignorant young man in love with at least the idea of the intellectual life, it was a thrillingly elevated* Reader's Digest. *The book's forbidding vocabulary and murderous syntax only increased my passion. It made it less likely that others would read it, and so I'd have what I wanted, exclusive superiority.*

*Toynbee was not the first world historian who'd shaken me. In the autumn of 1948, I sat in on H. R. Hughes's course in the culture and politics of modern Germany. Hughes lectured on Spengler, and I went off the rails of my M.A. in literature to read* The Decline of the West. *I haven't dared go back to it, as I have, say, to the other great literary passion of that year,* Remembrance of Things Past. *I must have sensed that Spengler's genius was more fragile than Proust's and that rereading it, with Toynbee and a few modest historians under my belt, might fracture the enchantment.*

*In 1951, I was living in Germany and had, a few months earlier, finished the last volume—published till then—of Toynbee's* Study *(borrowed from the Amerika Haus library in Heidelberg). When we moved to Frankfurt in May, I asked the director of the Amerika Haus there if I could lecture on the book. Since at least one special event had to be scheduled every night of the week except Sunday at the Amerika Haus, the director was grateful for anybody who'd be willing to fill an hour of program time. I wrote the piece more or less as it appears here. Here it's followed by the letter I received from Toynbee after I sent him a copy of it.*

As it is used in modern vernaculars, the word "history"— *l'histoire, Geschichte, storia, historia*—means the recording, certifying, and arranging of certain public events in a sequence which sustains, if possible, a conviction of causality. Although Toynbee's *Study of History* is a good deal more than this, it is also a good deal less than that total conception of the past which is often taken as the province of a "universal" view of history. History is *the story of what's happened;* the story includes recurrences and patterns. It's somewhat like the published diary of a conscientious, well-integrated person. Its aim is that of deepening the understanding; its means, arousing awareness of trends which can be endowed with living characteristics independent of the lives which have created and been consumed by them.

Oswald Spengler said that world history is *"der Ausdruck eines Formgefühls."* ("The expression of a feeling for form.") He was aware of the danger of pronouncing on totality from a position within it. I think his error lay in making the pronouncement without giving an adequate account of his position there. The tenor of his work groups him with Hegel and his disciples, and, in another sense, with Augustine and his as a prophet rising from the foam of his own enthusiasm. This student of Goethe hadn't taken to the lesson of *Faust*, that theology, law, magic, and devilry were insufficient to explain individual experience.

Another student of Goethe did learn this lesson, and his masterpiece, *A Study of History*, reveals the methodology worked out to embrace it. His "capacity for feeling form" was not damaged by the delusion that form was truth. Neither did he believe that only in the smallest area could enough evidence be marshaled to defeat the specter of completeness, of "totality."

The comparative failures of Acton and Mommsen, and the comparative successes of Spengler and, in a different measure, H. G. Wells, were Arnold Toynbee's stimuli. Observing the formers' timorous courting of *conclusive* evidence as an aspect of the "division of labor" element of the Industrial Revolution, and the parochial wooing of national brides by the majority of other nineteenth-century historians under the influence of the second major institution of the modern Western world, Nationalism, Toynbee followed Spengler and Wells by attempting to equate his single view with history in a marriage of equals. This commitment to the "long view" was controlled by what he called "units of intelligibility." These are the basis of his study. Once they're accepted, more or less everything follows. They allow him to make individual errors without endangering his basic conceptions.

Toynbee's "unit of intelligibility" is what he calls "civilization" or "society," words he partially equates with Spengler's *Kultur*. Civilizations are the smallest historical integers requiring minimal reference to each other. They arise in response to certain challenges of medial severity offered by environmental penalizations (such as the Tigris-Euphrates basin offered the Sumerians) or social pressure (the waves of the Minoan *Völkerwanderung* breaking on the Hellenes). Responses to the challenges which face civilization are led by creative personalities who convince a creative minority to charm the masses into imitation of successful responses. (Under the duress of population growth, Solon persuaded the Athenians to practice intensive cultivation. This led to Athens's becoming the "education of Hellas.") Creative personalities mature during a withdrawal from the social field but only become significant and complete by returning to that field. (Solon spent a year away from Attica learning the techniques of mercantilism. Arnold Toynbee devoted six years to war work before returning to write the last volumes of *A Study of History*.) After a period of growth characterized by a shifting and "etherialization" of the areas or nature of activity (the substitution of mechanical for motor traction; the simplification of scripts), a civilization becomes intoxicated

36

by its own triumphs and begins to decline. (The transformation of the Delian League into the Athenian Empire led to the Peloponnesian Wars.) The decline expresses itself in a loss of purpose and unity which leads to the formation of three groups, an External Proletariat (the barbarian war bands on the fringe of the Roman Empire), an Internal Proletariat (the Christians who carried the seeds of the new affiliated civilization in the Interregnum between civilizations), and a Dominant Minority, the tyrannical mask of what had been the Creative Minority (the Roman *equites* after the Hannibalic War). Civilizations usually decline in a rhythm of three disasters which alternate with three recoveries, and perish in a final disaster (the battle of Actium in 31 B.C.; A.D. 69, the year of the four emperors; the Interregnum beginning with the reign of Marcus in 180 and through that of Diocletian in 184; and the final rout in 378, the battle of Adrianople). Recoveries are led by "saviors." Saviors like Augustus and Napoleon establish Universal States. The real saviors *of* society are saviors *from* society. They are the saviors who inspire the higher religions of the universal churches. It is the hope of Western Society that although it has already entered its Time of Troubles (in the wars between the decline of the Italian city-states and the founding of the brief *pax oecumenica* of Napoleon), its Savior is the only one of the "Great Gods Incarnate in Man" who returned to the world as a sacrifice to his own beloved creation ("God so loved the world . . ."). Western Society's return to this Savior might mean its release from the suicidal patterns of the other civilizations.

Critics who see this conclusion as a lyric gasp irrelevant and even antithetic to the sweep of *A Study of History* ignore what can be seen even in the almost parodic summary given above, that formal provision has been made for what seems to be a belief of the author which did not arise inductively from empirical study. Christ has his historical position (the Savior of the Interregnum period) which formally allows for his potential as a "super-historical possibility."

There is another Toynbeean practice which both opens and closes the door to lethal criticism. This is his use of imagery.

37

Imagistic suggestions are not open to historical criticism because they represent a departure from the vocabulary in which such criticism must be couched. Facts are deniable, interpretations disputable, but one can only disagree with the artistic taste of chosen images.*

The question is how much historical interpretation can be metaphorical. Toynbee asks, "Is God to be prohibited by a human veto from revealing Himself through *Dichtung* as well as *Wahrheit?* Are not all human modes of expression at God's disposal?" He quotes Newman's famous phrase "the economy of truth" to indicate God's dispensation of reality through revelation and of revelation through reality. This suggests that not only are interpretative relationships (a comparison between the Tsin-Han dynasty and the Roman Empire) exercises in imagery, but the very *factuality* of these empires themselves is but an epiphenomenon of the interpreting force coursing through them.

A further question deals with the shaping of Toynbee's history by his abilities, inclinations, special knowledge and position. His "position" is that of a twentieth-century, upper-middle-class, academic English (Western) Christian. His abilities include linguistic competence, tremendous learning, and creative genius as measured by the ability to organize an enormous mass of fact and theory. He knows more about—at least is able to talk more about—literature than sculpture, painting, music, or dance. As for his disposition, one might call it traditional (though not conservative) and evangelical (rather than pious).

A Westerner, Toynbee values endeavor and action more than contemplation and passivity. So saviors are superior to great personalities who do not return to the world, and so the "growth" of civilization is more important than its ripening. (The Eskimos were "arrested" not because of mechanical primitivism but be-

---

*Freud said that he used the libido as a chemist does the elements and the physicist other units in the investigation of the "same" phenomenon. On the other hand, Hegel was convinced that because the vocabulary of his philosophy of history was equivalent to that of his logic that the completeness of the latter implied surety in the former. In other words, he identified his formal analysis of process with the natural operations of history.

cause of the monotony of the response they've made to the challenge of climate.)

As an (unorthodox) Christian, Toynbee believes that there is an end to the cyclic activity of the world.

Trained in the Latin and Greek "classics," he draws on the best documented of all early civilizations. These become his models. The interpretation, illustration, and literature of the Hellenic civilization take up a "disproportionate amount of space" in this world history. (An effect of this was cited in a well-known critique by Professor Pieter Geyl of Amsterdam, who said that if Toynbee's work is suspect in the field he knows best, what can we think of his analysis of Babylonia or the leavings of the Andes?)

A general proposition can be drawn here: the relationship between the factual and interpretative matter in a work creates a density which constitutes one's sense of its reliability. Is Toynbee's *Study* truer for Periclean Athens than for the Egyptian Third Dynasty? Are his notions applicable to Sumeria as well as Rome? When he elaborates the Aeschylean theme, *pathei mathos* (when, for example, its reverse, *suffering through learning,* is as useful), does it slight, say, Indian asceticism?

Toynbee's bias for literature leads to the slighting of other artistic triumphs as signs of plenitude. For example, the musical greatness of the West from Monteverdi to the present does not fit on Toynbee's graph of Western bloom and decay. And, too, the civilization-crossing lines of the Hagia Sophia or the influence of Arabian mathematics and philosophy are not aligned with those Toynbee prescribes for the contacts between civilizations.

Toynbee's skills lead to brilliant treatments of *lingua franca* and script. On the other hand, there are almost none of the wonderful comparisons of, say, Greek geometry, history, and sculpture which enliven Spengler's pages.

As for Toynbee's traditional, semi-evangelical tendencies, I think they help place Toynbee with the second generation of twentieth-century genius, a sibling of Mann rather than Joyce, Heisenberg rather than Einstein, Bartok rather than Schoenberg,

Jung and Lenin rather than Freud and Marx. The second group may be said to hold in common the exciting text that intelligibility is found in the fracture of the familiar and the creation of forms which limit what one can demonstrate. Toynbee does not startle us as much as thinkers who are not necessarily greater than he. His terminology, for instance, seems to be chosen to dampen the "flame which leaps from mind to mind": "Challenge and Response"; "Time of Troubles"; "New Wine in Old Bottles"; these suggest the stale talk of an Oxford High Table. Nor is his traditionalism that of seasonal recurrence but of a heavily-laden ship putting in at a nearer, less-exotic port.

Steady pursuit of an adversary insures triumph but requires a stamina that not only exhausts the quarry but impairs the grace of capture. *"Tantus labor non sit cassus"* ("So much labor can't be in vain") sits on the final page of Volume Six. Perhaps Paul Valéry's criticism of Pascal can be made of Toynbee: the gasp of terror before the infinite spaces and the quick resort to the salvationary antithesis is premature. The marriage smells of the shotgun.

*November 15, 1951*

Dear Mr. Stern,

Many thanks for your letter of the 28th October enclosing the copy of your paper, which naturally interested me very much.

I am aware, of course, of the two planes in my approach to history, to which you draw attention. This division is not, of course, exactly deliberate. I suppose I have always thought in this dual way as far back as I can remember. I am sure I have been deeply influenced by Plato's use of myths, and also to some extent by the two planes of action in Thomas Hardy's "The Dynasts".

When I started work on the book twenty or thirty years ago, I was rather remote from religion and have been continually surprised to find myself coming back towards it. As a matter of fact, if I were examined on orthodoxy I should be condemned on all the major doctrinal points in all the major religions.

One thing that strikes me is the poverty of human language. We have to make the same vocabulary do duty for quite different purposes, and we are fairly well used to the idea that words as used in poetry or fairy tales must not be construed as if they were being used in a work of science, but all the theologians have laboured to obscure the difference in the meaning of words when used to express religious truths and when used to express scientific truths, and this confusion has still to be disentangled.

Thank you again for sending me your paper. As you will see through these rather disjointed notes of mine, I was much interested in it.

Yours sincerely,

Arnold Toynbee

# *THE STORY OF ADELE H.*

The story of Adele Hugo is beautiful and heartrending. Crippled by the celebrity, genius, and unremitting tenderness of her father, the great poet, she tried for an independent life, first in music, then in that French art of despair, love. Her amorous genius poured over one Lt. Pinson, a cold and mendacious social climber. She followed him to Canada, then to the Barbados, dashing herself into madness on his rejections, and ending as an icon of *folie d'amour.*

A marvelous story, at least for biography or fiction, since the fascination is psychological. Which was perhaps what piqued François Truffaut.

Fresh from making *Day for Night,* a totally charming and totally filmic movie about his true love, making movies, Truffaut, driven by a *folie du cinema,* tried to cut a notch in the Bergman/Dryer pistol. In these years of unchained women, what better subject than a woman chained by the oldest of chains? And in these years of cinematic nostalgia—*The Wild Child, Godfather II, Barry Lyndon, McCabe and Mrs. Miller, The Magic Flute*—it's back to history for another run at deMille's costumed world.

There is more than a consonant between visual medium and visual tedium. The movies' heart is drama, not painting. A non-stop—undramatic—slide into obsession, no matter how scenic or *authentic,* won't work. Opera can get away with it if a Mozart writes the music. The mind is bewitched by the ear. The eye is

42

less powerful. It can't mesmerize the brain with ninety minutes of cobblestoned streets and prop-like actors. Mlle. Adjani turns Comédie-Française excess into furniture; she's little more than a talking couch.

Some of the world's worst decisions are made by vengeful geniuses. Truffaut, the fatherless ex-schoolboy, revenged himself on these father-ridden daughters of Victor Hugo—*"l'une pareille au cygne, et l'autre à la colombe"*—about whom his professors made him learn.

Asked who France's greatest poet was, André Gide made the famous answer, "Alas, Hugo." Alas, Truffaut's first dull picture fulfilled the poet's deathbed vision of *"lumière noire." Adele H.* is his *Night for Day.*

# COUNTRY FIDDLERS, CITY SLICKERS:
# VIRTUOSI AND REALISTS

Novels take off from any and everything, but novelists are mostly either virtuosi or realists. That is, they either aim at the remarkable, or organize what they feel about more or less imagined *familiar* experience until, because of their narrative gift, it seems remarkable to others. The virtuoso takes off from other writers' works. His virtuosity strikes the eye immediately: his language is different, the arrangement of it is different. We feel the eloquence, farce, fantasy, and technical mastery of his work. The realist focuses on what's *there* or could be. The realist wants his work to seem real.

Compare Cubists and Impressionists. The Cubists were virtuosi: they weren't interested in reordering the "real" and very little of it can be seen through their artistic glasses. (Though Picasso, to defend his earliest Cubist paintings, produced photographs of the rooftops of Horta, the town in which he'd painted them.) Their work, however, became part of the world, new actualities, like new varieties of melon. The Impressionist works are part of the world also, but they began as new prescription lenses. They altered—and still alter—ways of seeing trees, dancers, ponds, umbrellas, railroad stations.

There are also virtuosi-despite-themselves. These are often among the greatest artists and innovators. Schoenberg wrote that he did not consciously try to be different (that is, he did not set out to be a virtuoso); he said he'd been thrown into a boiling sea in which he had to make for shore without regard to the style of his stroke. Contrast this with my colleague Easley Blackwood and his work with new musical tunings. Like such literary experimenters as Robbe-Grillet and John Barth, Blackwood uses the word *exhaustion* to describe the condition of his art. He says the old musical material is exhausted; we've heard most of what can come of it; it's time for a new musical matter out of which composers will create new music. The theoretical virtuoso—Blackwood, Robbe-Grillet—works up his theory first. Sometimes it is in the form of a blueprint which he follows more or less mechanically. Barth told me—not totally for amusement—that the chief difficulty he had writing *Giles Goat-Boy*—once he'd worked up the scheme—was finding the right combination of stimulants to keep him awake at his typewriter.

Schoenberg's innovation came, I think, out of another process. Like the work of Kafka and Beckett, his innovations derived from expressive necessity. They themselves were not the necessity. Nor were they the expression of a need to be or appear original. I don't mean that powerful work can't come from a virtuoso's technical decisiveness, only that such work is rarely as fine as work which was blocked till the artist found new devices for realizing it.

Of course no *description* of an artist's process is very close to the process itself. Yet much literary process goes, I think, something like this: one works awkwardly toward a work, that is, toward a whole composed of certain events, themes, developments, scenes, or whatever engages the fictional energy. The assemblage is not easy. It has to make sense, it has to please the assembler. The result is sometimes strange. The more diverse the matter, the more striking the form of the ensemble (even when the whole seems real). One book revolves around imaginary letters, another around a confession, a third about a shattered and irrecoverable history. In my experience (which includes that of writers to whom I've talked), the work gets written once the mode of telling the story becomes inseparable from it.

Many realist writers have virtuoso impulses. They think of a method of doing a novel before they have any notion of subject matter. Or they conceive of a way of doing a particular subject which itself doesn't interest them. ("I want to write a novel about gray," said Flaubert.) The chief interest is the method. I think that most such notions come to nothing. You put in many hours pursuing what fails to excite you enough to continue. It's very hard to transform what may be what we can call a basic narrative temper.

Similarly, virtuoso writers usually come a cropper in straighter modes. (The straighter fiction in Barth's *Lost in the Funhouse* is not his best work.) On the other hand, some writers with essentially mimetic gifts sometimes bury the gift to pursue what they believe is the proper theoretical course. (For me, Michel Butor's best work is the essentially realist *Degrés* and Robert Coover's is his "realist" first novel, *The Origin of the Brunists.**)

*1985. I've changed my mind. I recently read his political farce, *The Public Burning*, and think it's wonderful. The realism, often a mass of historical fact, constitutes the powder which the farcical fury ignites. The brilliant stories of T. Coraghesson Boyle (cf. *Descent of Man and Other Stories*, 1979) are other marvelous, semi-realistic growths of the Joycean tree. Boyle writes variations on newsworthy themes. The variations are extravagant, passionately literary—that is, the love of verbal pyrotechnics is at least as great as love for the exposure, revelation, treatment (demolition or apotheosis) of the event or type of event which is the story's ostensible subject—and usually musically beautiful. The Flann O'Brien of *At-Swim Two Birds* is the closest post-Joycean to such work, though such Beckett work as *"Premier Amour"* is related to it. A fuller examination would contrast this work with some of Kafka's. A close reading of "The Country Doctor" (*"Ein Landarzt"*) will show the craziness within the apparent simplicity of the story. There is the usual Kafka dream-tempo, the leaps from place to place, subject to subject, but there is also the hardly conscious transformation of the doctor into the patient, the attack into the complaint, the descriptive into the lyric moan. Kafka would be a tough nut for this essay's thesis to crack. And all these writers would not serve those thinkers who claim that the contemporary, particularly "the contemporary American writer adds more and more images, more narrative, more 'characters,' more words—however rundown—to cover up the emptiness at the foundations of his construction—an emptiness he fears." These fear-ridden Americans are contrasted with such French writers as the tedious Blanchot and—the Pope of Disguised Amorous Kitsch—Mme. Duras, who are compared to sculptors "constantly [moving] around the material to be formed, never staying in one position very long, removing more and more material in order to create a shape . . . an extreme emptying out of images, narrative, character and words [you bet!] in order to reach their silent, but solidly significant core—an erotic core that [they] can then embrace." Alice Jardine, *Gynesis* (Ithaca: Cornell University Press, 1985), p. 235.

Writers who evade their own gift often produce the most distended and tedious work. ("The Unreadable Book" is a modern genre.)

I myself have wasted months on such ideas as: (1) a novel arranged alphabetically, characters being taken up in the order of the spelling of their names, the novel developing by thickening the connections of the apparently unconnected persons; (2) a narrative in the form of a computer conference in which conferees enter at any point of the basic discussion by appending their contribution to the appropriate, numbered section (the idea was to create an interlocked narrative out of apparently heterogeneous materials); (3) a narrative in which different elements of narration itself relate the story over or through the author's head. So "Voice," "Plot," and "Subject" make their very peculiar narrative claims. Of the hundreds of pages and hours devoted to this enterprise only four pages—printed at the end of the volume *1968*—survive. The others are part of the Himalaya of wastage in my closet.

A geneticist friend told me about something called a *nonsense mutant*. Professor Robert Edgar named these forms of genetic material which contain segments that make no sense to the reduplicating molecules and thus mark the end of the line. However, Professor Edgar then went on to discover so-called suppressors of the nonsense mutants, that is, certain proteins which made sense of the nonsense and thus enabled genetic continuance. For me, most virtuoso work can be compared to such nonsense mutants, interesting perhaps in themselves, but as sports, as more or less attractive *culs-de-sac*. Now and then, though, such sports will be picked up by very different sorts of writers who will be able to transform their own work and thus continue the literary line. Joyce took—so he said—the internal monologues of Dujardin's *Les lauriers sont coupés* and employed them in the brilliant monologues of *Ulysses;* and Flaubert, his own "suppressor," took the notion of "received ideas" from his *Dictionary of Received Ideas* and employed it in the narrative comedy of the druggist Homais and the farcical entrepreneurs, Bouvard and Pécuchet.

# The Position of the Body

I want to speculate about a different but related matter. It strikes me that most of the leading contemporary American virtuosi are Gentiles. The American-Jewish fiction of the post-World War II years is basically realistic. This has not always been the case, and it is not the case in other countries. Now, though, it seems that in this country the best-known virtuosi of narrative fiction are non-Jews: Barth, Barthelme, Coover, Gass, Hawkes, Purdy, and Pynchon (though he may be more of a realistic fantasist than a conscientious virtuoso). Why are such distinguished Jewish writers as Bellow, Elkins, Harris, Mailer, Malamud, Roth, and Salinger more or less straightforward writers?

I can think of some explanations. Almost all the Jews are urban, most of the non-Jews small-town or country boys. Perhaps the urban writer is so bombarded by variety that, very early, he knows his job is to make sense of it, while the country writer dreams or fantasizes his way out of a familiar, comparatively static order. The urban writer's problem is making sense out of heterogeneity; the country writer's is the conjuration of something beyond familiar homogeneity.*

In art, virtuosity is linked with dream, with evasion, and with escape. From Chamisso (author of *Peter Schlemiel*), a French *evadé*, through Nabokov, refugees from revolution have taken to narrative fantasy. Of the leading post-World War II Jewish writers, only three, Singer, Wiesel, and Schwartz-Bart, are, I believe, refugees, and their work veers into fantasy. (Malamud, an occasional refugee of the spirit, was also—"The Jew-Bird"— an occasional fantasist.)

Psychic turbulence may precipitate the same sort of conspicuously ordered, virtuosic structures as political turbulence. The disturbed writer reaches for every means of control, as sociopaths do in life. (Until they explode, they are usually the best of quiet citizens.)** So—to take essentially non-literary exam-

---

*Of his long periods of seclusion in the Esterházy summer palace, Haydn told his biographer Griesinger: "I was cut off from the world—there was no one to confuse or torment me, and I was forced to become original."

**The very conservative politician is frequently a person whose need for public order helps control a disturbed interior.

48

ples—the adventurous fantasies of an Ian Fleming, the sophisticated craft and dream play of a Strindberg, or the technical mastery of Orson Welles derive from serious, if not pathological, displacement.

Is there anything else in Jewish experience common to the twenty or thirty leading American Jewish writers which bends them toward realistic rather than virtuoso fictions?

My guess is that the realist feels a confidence born of the possibility of overcoming an eccentric social position. Virtuosity may derive from the despair of displaced insiders. (Indeed, this may be the trigger of most literary experience from Homer's on.) Given the temperamental extremes in writers—their individuality is nourished by articulating the specialness of their temperaments—they are nonetheless a class, a group with common characteristics. They are active people whose professional activity is physically restrictive. They use the most flexible, most easily dominated artistic medium, words, and encounter next to no physical restriction—no paint, marble, canvas, dancers' bodies, wood and catgut, actors' temperaments. They are thus artistically *spoiled;* they can indulge themselves with what pleases only them. If they are haters of the philistines who surround them, they can revenge themselves by writing works that are conspicuously impenetrable. (In a city, one is less likely to be immersed in ignorance and philistinism.)

Is it fair to say that all but the most-benighted Jewish families maintain respect for the *book,* for the *learned man,* the *writer*? Many burgher Jewish fathers don't want their children to be writers, but still usually respect books. In a community where every ounce of energy must be productive, this is not often the case. *

I once got a letter from a writer, David Martin, whose first novel, *Tethered* (Holt, Rinehart and Winston, 1979), is about growing up in a small Illinois agricultural town. He went back to his home town for Christmas, and one of his unamiable high school friends talked to him about the book. The fellow hadn't

---

*The case of country aristocrats who, for much of civilization, constitute the majority of writers, is another matter.

read or probably seen it, but he knew that a book authored by his old acquaintance existed. When Martin came by, the fellow was disembowelling a hog. His critical comment consisted of slicing out the hog's anus and tossing it to Martin. It would be hard to match this experience in New York or Chicago. (Nor are there that many Jewish farmers around—though some prosperous Jewish authors may list themselves as farmers on tax forms.)*

Most of the Jewish writers I know come from families which were actively melting into the great American pot. The family direction was Americanization, that is, movement toward open-ended prosperity and full acceptance. Newcomers to games usually play by the rules. Is it too much to say that the novel-writing children of these new Americans tended to play by narrative rules? Their books—filled with an American experience which usually ended in either triumph or bittersweet loss—toe, often brilliantly, the realistic narrative line.

For a time, after World War II, Jewish and Gentile writers wrote the satiric, angrily farcical works that are called "black humor." Often their eye was on the war, a phenomenon whose maniacal orderliness was a kind of public virtuosity. For the writers, what counted was the *object out there*, not the method of presentation. So even such virtuosic-looking books as *Catch-22* were essentially realistic. It would not be easy to distinguish

*One distinguished Jewish author became a chicken farmer after he found that literature couldn't support him: Henry Roth, author of the wonderful *Call It Sleep*. Incidentally, a contemporary of Roth's, Daniel Fuchs, recently (*Chicago Tribune Bookworld*, Nov. 3, 1985) wrote that as far back as 1935, critics were complaining about the excess of "Jewish novels." He cited John O'London's *Weekly*, Sept. 21, 1935: "They are becoming rather too many and too much alike." Twenty-six years later, the same publication put the dour face of an English cleric above a review of my own first novel. A week later, they printed a letter from Leslie, bishop of Lincoln, to the effect that every man was entitled to a copyright of his own features, however dismal they might be. He despaired of Mr. Stern's reaction to the association of his name with such features. Of course, I was delighted, and delighted, too, that another reader noted that the *Weekly* had played its own "golk." Now it occurs to me that this publishing *lapsus* might be worth a few lines in a revised edition of *The Psychopathology of Everyday [Literary] Life*.

such books by the social or religious backgrounds of their authors: the army is the truest melting pot.

## BUSINESS CODA

In the palmy, postwar period of American publishing, federal and foundation funds subsidized library purchases, and publishers allowed new talent a couple of failed or marginal novels before they ran out its string. (I myself was generously indulged by publishers who for years lost money on my work.) The richness of post-World War II American writing, both realistic and virtuosic, is as clearly related to such munificence as the Elizabethan drama was to the prosperity of audiences enriched, as well as excited, by the voyages of discovery. This palmy time is long gone. Conglomerate publishing has distended the modes of salesmanship: television advertising creates publishing expense which necessitates enormous sales; proportionately fewer good novels are published, so that the few which are will have the bookstore space needed to redeem the expense. What effect such constriction will have on the mental life of the nation remains to be seen. The menace is of a continued narrowing of taste and a shrinkage in the individuality which has for two hundred and fifty years been both invented and nurtured in fiction.

# ON SHORT STORIES

*The short story, as a product, perhaps even as a formative con-*
*dition, of human society, is, I'd guess, the oldest of narrative art*
*forms. Buried by the novel in the nineteenth and very early*
*twentieth centuries, it came back strong in the twenties, and now,*
*in the last decades of this century, it's once again one of the most*
*sophisticated art forms of the West. It's not just that people can*
*satisfy their hunger for narrative quickly, it's that increasing so-*
*phistication breeds aesthetic hunger for compression, ellipsis, ob-*
*liquity, and rapidity. A sophisticated culture needs fewer*
*preparations and signals, less supporting data and conclusive dem-*
*onstration. Post-Mondrian—Minimalist—painting, post-Bran-*
*cusi sculpture, post–Webern music, these arts rise from the same*
*mind-set as the laser and silicon chip. The short stories of Ray-*
*mond Carver, Mary Robison, Tobias Wolff, Amy Hempel, Bette*
*Pesetsky, Ann Beattie,\* and twenty or twenty-five other brilliant*

---

\*In a review of Beattie's novel, *Love Always*, John Updike compared her procedure with Hemingway's: "It was she who first found the tone for the post-
Vietnam, post-engagé mood, much as Hemingway found the tone for his own
generation's disenchantment with all brands of officially promoted importance.
Both authors made reality out of short, concrete sentences and certifiable, if small,
sensations; in the absence of any greater good, the chronic appearance of food
on the table becomes an event worth celebrating." I don't think Beattie is the first
New Minimalist—quite a few roasted the leaner meat of the fifties and sixties before the Beatties and Carvers worked up the soybean, meatoid versions of the
seventies and eighties—but Updike, himself one of the fine chefs of the oldtime
roasts and gammons, is, I think, right about their recipes and ancestry.

*masters of surface realism are the most recent American exempla
of this understated, bare, deceptive, and rather chilly art. They
are not poetic parodists like Donald Barthelme or Jorge Luis
Borges; they are not tragic, philosophic farceurs like Beckett;
they're not experimentalists like Sarraute, Barth, and Robbe-
Grillet. They are American realists in the line of Sherwood Anderson and his treacherous disciple, Hemingway. Although I adore
many of their stories, my own preference—and practice—is for
fuller, more richly detailed ones. Bellow is the greatest recent
story writer in this line, and it may be that his art is more
conspicuous in the long story than in the novel, simply because
he's had to find ways to control his desire to comment about
everything. Newer masters, though, are the Barry Hannah of*
Airships *and the Bobbie Ann Mason of* Shiloh. *John Cheever,
Peter Taylor, J. F. Powers, Philip Roth, John Updike, Bernard
Malamud, and Flannery O'Connor are other post-World War II
masters of the full story. It's foolish, though, to cite a few names.
Almost every fine modern writer has written wonderful short
stories. In this section, I comment on four of them.*

### HESSE'S STORIES

Thomas Mann told a young American writer* that when he
and his brother began writing in the 1890s, "we had to do it all
ourselves." He meant that German fiction had had no Balzac,
Gogol, or Fielding. It had not taken a grip on society but had
shuttled between the dream tales of Novalis and the little-burgher
rusticity of Gottfried Keller. Helped by—of all things—Wagner's treatment of three generations in his Ring operas, Mann
performed the Balzac/Flaubert/Zola graft on German literature
in one operation, *Buddenbrooks* (1901).

Two years younger than Mann, Herman Hesse began writing
under his almost lifelong deference to Mann's superior power.

---

*In 1951, I had a long lunch with Katia and Thomas Mann in Bad Gastein.
Much of what the great man said I later read in his little book, *Die Entstehung
des Dr. Faustus.*

# The Position of the Body

(Mann graciously accepted the deference and graciously reciprocated with praise of Hesse.) Male artists often function as twin stars: Picasso/Braque, Stravinsky/Schoenberg, Wordsworth/Coleridge, Eliot/Pound, Sartre/Camus. These pairs remain conscious of each other's work, attempt what the artistic twin hasn't, answer questions raised by their twin's accomplishment. With Mann's playful, sensuous, ironic power twirling beside him in literary space, Hesse followed that un-Mannian part of his nature which, every twenty years or thirty years, has turned him into the Pied Piper of the reading young.* In 1974, Hesse's publishers issued a selection of his stories under a Mannian title.**

Like Byron or Solzhenitsyn, Hesse is more remarkable as a human being who writes than as a sheer writer. His work is a series of trails into self-discovery and self-transcendence. The trails are journeys east, up and in; to India and Indian thought (with *Siddhartha* as the great trek); to Swiss mountains, where, behind No Visitor plaques, Hesse read, translated, edited, and invented tales about the world's sages; and then inwards, for, in a manner hearts calloused by fact can neither comprehend nor enjoy, Hesse suffered and expressed crises of doubt about himself, his country, and about ways of knowing anything. Psychoanalyzed by a Jungian, divorced, exiled, he moved further and further away from Europe's civil life, a learned, spirited, gentle cultivator of gardens and instincts, a seeker after ecstasy and revelation, a writer who wanted to be a seer but remained a professional man of letters who—like most others of worth—often doubted his literary powers.

The twenty-three stories in the collection (all but three new to English readers) were written between 1899 and 1948 (the year after he won the literary Good Housekeeping Seal, the

---

*In 1974, eighty percent of my sophomore and junior students said they'd read some of his work. Eleven years later, it's down to fifty percent, but as the literary market goes, that's not bad.

**Stories of Five Decades. New York: Farrar, Straus & Giroux. (Mann's are collected as *Stories of Three Decades*. The amiable rivals tussle beyond the grave.)

Nobel Prize). In them, one can trace a career more absorbing than any single literary version of it.

Not that there aren't good stories here. There is, for instance, a three-page account of the creation, growth, decay, and forest-burial of "The City," as beautiful and much richer than Marcel Marceau's sixty-second mimicry of the ages of man; there's a story of a merchant's return to the mean Swabian town where he delicately courts a slandered widow; there's another about an English missionary whose desire for a bare-breasted Indian girl alters his mission.

Many stories are charged with that leaden servitude to suppressed sensuality which is the forerunner of so much mysticism and mischief. The finest stories are the barest and most direct, or so it seems to a modern reader who wants stories which say, "You know I'm true because I'm hiding nothing."

To younger truth-seekers, Hesse's line is the shortcut to Ecstasy. Yet, looked at closely, his trips aren't easy. In the tiny story "Edmund," a student of Indian tantras meditates on the text.

> If you find yourself in a situation where your soul falls sick and forgets what it needs for life . . . then make your heart empty . . . perceive the center of your head as an empty cave . . . and concentrate on the contemplation of it. Then the cave will . . . show you an image of what your soul needs in order to go on living.

Edmund follows the prescription, sees where his salvation lies and, "with joyful certainty," strangles his professor.

"Etherial as a dream, exact as a logarithm." This is how Hesse described Kafka in 1925. Kafka was that fusion of Mann and Novalis, storyteller and seer, which Hesse wanted to and knew he couldn't be.

> Only at long last . . . he realised that he must content himself with being a true poet, a dreamer, a seer, only in his soul, and that his handiwork must remain that of a simple man of letters.
>
> "Dream Journeys"

# The Position of the Body

No mean thing, though it didn't satisfy Hesse. Still, for young questers, there is a Hessian blue in the world which would not exist if Herman Hesse had not been for fifty years a working man of letters.

## MARY ROBISON'S *DAYS*

Dick trims his nails and sniffles about one of his ex-wives who lives in the Oldsmobile his parents gave them. His mother reads and listens to a tape of *Porgy and Bess.* Dick's brother, Spencer, sunbathes in a nylon lounge chair while his father hoses the driveway (spraying Spencer). A young woman, seven months pregnant, passes out a flyer about a school bond issue. Spencer tells her the economy's collapsing, "there'll be a global depression by 1990." Summoned into the house, he sticks the blue flyer on his chest. His mother tells him he looks fit, tells Dick he's very attractive, tells them both their father is the pregnant woman's OB. Upstairs, Spencer puts a cordovan loafer on Dick's foot and buffs it with a yellow cloth. They hear their parents laughing.

"What are they laughing about?" Spencer said.
"I wouldn't know," said Dick. "Probably not about us."

End of story. Four pages. Twenty-three hundred words, title "Doctor's Sons."

The modern short story, brief, oblique, epiphanic, was invented, or better, tripped into, by the young medical student Anton Chekhov in the early 1890s. Its complex telegraphy—*micrography?*—is one of the premier art forms of the century.

Since the art is that of exclusion, the pressure is to keep excluding, the menace that of stripping down to the skeletal, the anecdotal, or even to a void signed in the philosophic bravado of Duchamp or Warhol. The reader has a right to ask, "If you've told the story in seven hundred words, what do the other sixteen hundred of the story do?"

Fair enough. The "other words" of "Doctor's Sons" give us the "linen placemat decorated with Coast Guard flags" on which

Dick's hands rest, the navel orange he bumps on the window to call his brother, and the pointed-pointless talk of the three Sorensons. That is, the words sustain a world of oranges, hoses, brothers, and loafers long enough so that we can ride the ups and downs of their uneasy comfort and feckless tension. "Doctor's Sons." The world of the doctor—of provisions, earning, Oldsmobiles, lawns, lounge chairs, loafers—and that of the sons, who loaf, lounge, tan their bodies, trim their nails, sweep, predict collapse, and know they bring no laughter to their parents. The four pages are the surface of an unwritten three hundred. (The unwritten chapters deal with Dick's wives, Spencer's world, a—perhaps—intrigue with the pregnant girl, the disintegration of what is momentarily suspended in the story.) The art and the joy are in our ability to pick up the signs of this sour world.

Narrative spareness concentrates the mind as a microscope does. And ordinary language increases a reader's desire to press meaning out of the bareness. So the words "lounger" and "loafer" stir small currents which would be beside the point in longer, "richer" stories. Generations of fine writers and alert readers lie behind such understanding. There are a few longer, richer, and more complicated stories in *Days*, but all twenty are made for lovers of obliquity and compression.

Social scientists could read this book for their purposes as well. There is much to learn about this 1970s America of comfortless comforts, one-parent children, ulcerous fifteen-year-olds, unhappy nuns, sudden punches or needs to punch. An oil painter's paints are clotted, he makes kites to fly as a hurricane blows up; ex-wives and husbands pester each other; a pretty girl provokes a fight amid the wreckage of a beach hotel; a woman rereads and abandons a sentence which begins, "I saw the Earth cower . . ." The stories unroll in Beverly Hills, Indianapolis, Cleveland, Philadelphia, Erie, Chicago. This ubiquity is itself social theory.


BARRY HANNAH'S *RAY*

*Ray* looks at first like such a wee pile of novel-fragments, I thought my pal Barry must have swept them together to keep up his morale and make himself remember he was a writer. Two years ago, he'd read its most inconsequential fragment to a Chicago group. He'd come up here in his green leather jacket, dark goggles, and the brown suit his wife had made him pack instead of the revolver he thought he'd need in these mean streets. To the audience, he played a borrowed trumpet to show he was only a fair musician, but a hell of a writer.

Which he is.

*Airships* was the best new book of short stories I'd read in years, and his two early novels, *Nightwatchmen* and *Geronimo Rex,* are also grand, lyric, surprising, and both big-hearted and mean. Pure Hannah.

As is *Ray,* this—if each word is wringing wet—*novella.* Twenty thousand words, which, oddly enough, give you the weight of a novel, everything you'll ever know about Doc Ray, his second wife Westy, her kids, his kids, his girl—Sister—her parents, the soap factory foreman and poet, Hooch, and his wife Agnes who "watches Home Box Office Movies, which cause her untold anguish for not being slim, twenty-three, in a black dress and pearls, with a sub-machine gun in her hands, in an old fort on the Mediterranean." Summarize the novel's events and you'll think it's a full-size affair. Which is part of the point.

Since the novel began, a few novelists have taken out its stuffing to purvey miniature, rapid or burlesque versions of it. *Tristram Shandy* (1759) and Machado Assis's *Epitaph of a Small Winner* (1880) are no twenty-thousand-word weaklings but full-grown with that sportive nonchalance which tells the reader, "You get the idea, I don't need to spell out all this old stuff." These novels spin around central characters who are as eccentrically selective as charm permits. Part of the pleasure is seeing how much they skip. If, here and there, a reader feels cheated (of the promised novel), the compensation is the lyric whirl of observation, the vigorous uproar of language.

> The land is full of crashing jets, carbon monoxide, violent wives, and murderous men. There is a great deal of metal and hardness.
>
> (*Ray*)

The heroes of these books often dream several lives at once.

First, I took the form of a Chinese barber . . . soon after I became . . . St. Thomas' *Summa Theologica* . . . .
(Epitaph of a Small Winner)

When Ray is not shooting up "gook jets" in Vietnam, he's
commanding Confederate cavalry in Maryland. "Oh, help me!
I am losing myself in two centuries and two wars." A doctor,
he's getting cured, probably in a loony bin. It hardly matters.
(The writer, inventing, is half there himself.) What matters is
that he lays out his lust, his scruples, his needs: to "duke a big
guy," to drop "the big one" on the States—especially Ohio, to
ravish—i.e., describe?—

a tall girl, twenty-six, and her legs are an amazing long event.
Beyond that, she's just a straight honest slut.

Despite provocation, temptation,

I never had her. It is a perversity. . . . I hired her just to tempt
myself and resist . . .

The prose, magical, tricky, lyric, comes out of that Mississippi
of great prose, post-World War II American fiction. There must
be a hundred novelists who can write magic.

He saw spacious skies and amber waves of grain. Most of all he
saw the alligator hummocks of Florida and, in his mind's eye, a
stately bat tower standing in an endless saw-grass savannah over
which passed the constant shadows of tropical cloudscapes; merry
bats singled out stinging bugs at mealtime; Payne confronted a
wall of Seminole gratitude.
(Thomas McGuane, The Bush-Whacked Piano)

Or, from a lesser-known writer, Paul Spike:

Tall as a Watusi, she seems. Dark brown hair flowing long, a
rich mane crossing the small elegant bust. A face which is deadpan
and wealth and front page.

(Bad News)

I think the source of this river may be Céline's *Voyage au
bout de la nuit*, published in France in 1932 but retranslated for
New Directions in 1960 amidst the *vendange* of black humor:

# The Position of the Body

After a moment of friendliness, I slithered up against her body. It was fine with the lantern on the ground, because you could catch at the same time the shifting reliefs of the light on her legs. Ah! Nothing must be missed of moments like that! One's cock-eyed with excitement. It's worth it every time. What a fillip, what sudden good humor overtakes you!

Even in translation, Céline's voice sounds real, that is, what a reader of Barry Hannah can recognize as being part of the day's world.

You may ask, "Are you citing these comparisons to make Hannah seem superfluous?"

Absolutely not.

You had a good dinner last night, but you want another tonight, n'est-ce pas? Music, flowers, your girl's mouth? These aren't once-in-a-lifetime events, I hope. That Hannah has cousins, parents, and will soon have sons and nephews doesn't mean he's not unique. He is, and even so tiny a scoopful of him as *Ray* is precious, unXeroxable, an intense and rereadable joy.

## KUNDERA

En route to a two-week vacation in Czechoslovakia's Tatra Mountains, a young man stops for gas. His shy girlfriend goes off to pee in the woods. Then she pretends to be a hitchhiker and flags down his car. The game intrigues him; he pretends she's a pickup. The pretense excites them. They turn off the road and check into a hotel. The shy girl strips with seductive confidence. The young man treats her like a whore. They lie in the dark. "I'm me," she says. "I'm me."

Milan Kundera's stories can't be read in Czech. This non-literary fact is somehow embedded in these stories and, in fact, in almost any writing that comes out of Eastern Europe. The Czech writer Vaculík writes about the "indulgent forbearance" with which he feels even sophisticated Western readers listen to the "eternal babbling about one thing" which comes out of Eastern writing. The counter to this is the tyrant's knowledge that good writing endangers the Penitentiary State. Even when stories deal with private lives, the setting becomes a large part of the story. In "The Hitchhiking Game," the setting tells us the lovers' usual lives are boring. That is, The State is boring. The reader of such stories knows that the unexpected is dangerous, that pleasure has to be reserved well in advance, and that a life is supposed to be exemplary rather than personal.

American literature swept the world not just as poems and stories but as a promise of possibility and variety. The stories of Eastern Europe smell of the ingenuities which human beings use to extract pleasure from the stinginess of a nagging state. "Today," writes Vaculík, "Ugly deeds are not characteristic of the prisons but rather of the tranquil civic existence of those who are not in prison."

They're part of literature as well, and not just the literature of hypocrisy, recantation, and betrayal. The very texture and form of Kundera's stories—the philosophic riddles like "Symposium," the cold farces like "Edward and God"—are triumphs of evasion as well as invention.

It is easier to run away for short periods. Novels are for the rare long-distance runner. (Solzhenitsyn's *The First Circle* is one of the few Eastern novels of sustained force.) Kundera's novel, *Life Is Elsewhere,* has some brilliant descriptions of a young poet's discovery of the odd powers of poetry and a good portrait of a woman's affair with an artist who uses her body as his canvas and her head as his classroom, but political anger breaks the book—becomes the book—and the stories dribble out. Kundera attempts to sustain them by making the poet all poets, but the snippets from Lermontov, Keats, Baudelaire, and Shelley water the book down.

Kundera is best at drawing out the farcical complexity of anecdote and situations. He's at his easiest in sexual comedy *(The Farewell Party),* his worst in high-falutin' lucubration *(The Unbearable Lightness of Being).* He doesn't have the tenacity—or is it the will?—to organize a long haul into a single situation or group of situations. But why punish him because he isn't Tolstoy or Graham Greene or his friend Philip Roth?

61

# BITTEN LIPS

*It seems to me appropriate at this point to give a short account
of Africa. . . . Concerning those regions and tribes which are
seldom visited because the country is hot or mountainous or
desert, I am not in a position to give any reliable information;
and the rest I shall deal with in the fewest possible words.*
     —*Sallust,* The Jugurthine War, *40* B.C.

*Surely, Shakespeare can speak Kinyawanda. He might not
understand some concepts and then he might bite his lips as we
do when we are learning to speak English, but he may
overcome many difficulties if he works hard.*
—*Ndwaniye Augustin, third-year student, National University
   of Rwanda, in* Echo from Ruhande *(Jan. 1981), IX,1*

*N'Gaoundere  18 April 1926*
*Nothing exotic in the landscape, which, however, seemed too
big for a France to contain it.*
     —*André Gide,* Le retour du Tschad, *1928*

# AMERICAN AND AFRICAN WINTERS: A FEW DISTANT GUESSES

*This is the original—English—version of a talk which my friend Françoise Meltzer (and her mother) put into French so that I could deliver it in francophone countries in North, West, and East Central Africa in the winter of 1981. If I'd written it after, rather than before the trip, I would have had more to say about what is mentioned in the "Excerpts from a Report," the bravery, if not crazy intrepidity it takes to be a writer in most of Africa. There'll be no African Balzac for many a year. When a good poem or story, let alone novel or play, is written there, the heroism as well as the gift of the writer should be celebrated. Talk of exile and cunning. Joyce's Ireland was Shakespeare's London compared to the situation in Cotonou, Lomé, Freetown, Rabat, and Nairobi (where the writer N'gugi was in jail during my stay, guilty of having produced a work of his in Gikiyu which excited ethnic and political passion in what the government hoped would be a politically passive group).*

As I write this, the first snow of the year is falling in Chicago. The eaves and roofs of the three-story brick and wooden houses are wigged with the piling crystals. I am sitting by the typewriter trying to figure out what would be of interest to my future friends and colleagues in Africa, and it occurs to me that the snow itself should play a part in it. So much of what I know and feel has been conditioned by these northern seasons: the annual retreat to overheated interiors, the expense of heat and

65

# The Position of the Body

shelter, the rhythms of winter—the first snow becoming the second, the third, the tenth, the Januaries and Februaries grinding down the souls of those who live here. (It is no accident that sees me coming to Africa in February. Escaping the winter here has become one of my aims.) I wonder how much of what separates south and north has to do with escape from the cold. On the one hand, there are the political and economic systems built upon the search for fuel, on the other, the mental expectations of the year—the excitement of the northern spring with its release of hibernating energy. How much passion, how many love affairs and how many wars begin in the northern April.

My own life is determined even more by the seasons than that. (I am a kind of urban farmer.) Like most American writers, artists, and composers, I pay the rent not by income from my art, but by teaching in a university. My year begins then not with January 1, the Feast of the Circumcision, but with the return of students to campus in late September. My mind and heart are conditioned to the academic schedule, to weekends, holidays, semester breaks, and the long summer vacation. If Shakespeare's mind was saturated with theater—" . . . my nature is subdu'd / To what it works in, like the dyer's hand"—how much of my poorer nature has been "subdu'd" by this university schedule? Is this like asking what I would be if I'd been born a Masai *moran* [warrior], or a woman? Still, I can offer some general answers about such things as the effect of the writing professors on twentieth-century literature.

First, of course, there are all the stories and novels about professors and students, novels of love and loss, May-and-December affairs; then there are the countless novels about academic and critical politics. This is too obvious to discuss. I'm more interested in a certain quality in the work of the artist-teachers of our time. I'll call the quality *speculative luxuriance.* Whether it is Munira, the protagonist of ex-Professor N'gugi's *Petals of Blood,* engaging in passionate reflection about murderous capitalism, or Kinbote, the mad critic of Professor Nabokov's *Pale Fire,* or Professor Saul Bellow's Mr. Sammler speculating about the decay of modern American cities, or Professor Jorge Luis Borges speculating about speculation itself, the authority, the voice, the mental rhythm of the literature is speculation and instruction. The instruction may be farcical or furious, parodic or pathetic. In the Americas, it is often ironic and sad, as if the voice behind the thought dare not offer something absolute or even clear.

If you'll permit a comment on my own longest work of this sort, a novel called *Other Men's Daughters*, I'll say that the emotional insecurity of my middle-aged hero was supposedly a contrast to his assurance about his own work as a physiologist. Yet the book is dominated by Professor Merriwether's persistent attempt at characterizing and interpreting almost everything he sees and feels. If he did not have what I have, the luxury of time for thought, neither he nor the novel would exist.

The books of this century, then, are as bookish in their way as those of the early eighteenth century. Those books floated on the often exciting fact of the book as book. How marvelous that you could write prefaces and footnotes, contradict yourself on the same page, using different editorial voices.

Our books are bookish in a deeper, more nervous way. I think they're marked by a hunger to catalog, to compare, to preserve. It is not just a matter of technology—the technology which produces comparatively inexpensive paperback libraries and museums of reproductions—or the surplus capital and tax systems which led to the creation of real museums and libraries. It has, I think, more to do with a sense on the part of most of us, particularly those of us who live and die by the book, that the fury of the modern spirit can, with the chill and the power of its weapons, send the whole show up in smoke. How fragile is our great urban culture of libraries, museums, universities, and concert halls. "There died a myriad," wrote Ezra Pound after World War I,

> And of the best, among them,
> For an old bitch gone in the teeth,
> For a botched civilization . . .

And what is that civilization?

# The Position of the Body

> . . . two gross of broken statues . . .
> a few thousand battered books.
> *(Hugh Selwyn Mauberley)*

Maybe those of us who train the young most fear that we're not only exhausting the materials of the earth, the minerals which house, and the old organic compounds which warm us, but the very attitudes and feelings which generations of novelists and psychologists have partly described, partly created. The referential, allusive quality of much modern work often comes out in parody and satire; beneath them lie fear, boredom, and contempt. "Is there nothing more to human beings than this old stuff?" say the professorial voices from the literary laboratories of France and the two Americas. Much of what we call modernity in this century has been this boredom with exposure and parody of antiquity. The *Odyssey* has given birth to more than one *Ulysses*. More Trojan wars have been fought on modern stages than classical ones.

The greatest writers of this century are thick with old texts; the works of some, such as Señor Borges, seem almost entirely composed of them. The brilliant comment on the matter can be found in his first great story, "Pierre Menard, Author of *Don Quixote*," in which a twentieth-century French symbolist devotes himself to writing two chapters of a seventeenth-century Spanish work which turn out to be, word for word, chapters from *Don Quixote*.

My African colleagues may feel that this little talk is itself the idling speculation of someone who comes from a culture of luxury. What I say may have no application at all to the situation of the African writer. If I can believe some things I have read, that is the case. So Ezekiel Emphahlele once said that the urgency of African life didn't allow for the luxurious development of a novel; only short stories were possible. This made me think of a most un-Emphahlele-like writer, Edgar Allan Poe, whose justification for the short story was not social, but aesthetic. His belief was that literature should transmit only pure sensations.

Since no writer could be pure for more than a few lines, then the short story and lyric poem were the only pure forms. (Such different urgencies behind the same end, one the product of speculative luxuriance, the other that of social *engagement*.) Then there is the Ghana poet and playwright Ama Ata Aidoo, who said that she envied Françoise Sagan's ability to write about lovers. "Who cares about lovers in Accra?" asked Miss Aidoo. Reading that, I nearly fell out of my chair. I wanted to cry out, "I care." But her point was Emphahlele's: "In Africa, there are more urgent things than love." From before Plato's time, this has been a refrain poets have been assailed by (or have adopted themselves, perhaps in the spirit of inoculation). It is both true and untrue. When it takes every ounce of energy to survive the day, who can pay attention to the look of a face, a taste of honey, or any feelings (except, perhaps, those of rage and pity, the parents of reform and progress)? On the other hand, what should the end of reform and progress be but the education of the sentiments?

A decade or so ago, the English critic A. Alvarez interviewed groups of American and Eastern European writers. He found that the complaints of American writers had to do with their psyches, their literary problems and, now and then, with the crassness of critics, publishers, and the public. The Eastern European writers talked hardly at all about such things. Their troubles were clear. They came from outside, from the great systems to which they had to adapt, either by conformity, by subtle evasion, or by summoning up resources of obduracy and resistance.

I am trying to learn what African writers of all sorts think about these matters today, yet I know that even back in the sixties, when Emphahlele and Ama Ata Aidoo spoke, there was a great range of opinion about the writer's relationship to his culture. The late Nigerian poet Christopher Okigbo sounded more like the average American than the average East European writer, except that the freedom of choice about which he talked was self-conscious and, perhaps because of that, more precious to him. It was not of his suspension between the world of the

69

village and the city or between animism and Christianity that he talked, but his ability to shuttle between them. "I can eat pounded yam at Nigeria House one day and lamb chops the next. I wear an Italian jacket. I'm not Italian, I'm an African. I wear a tie and I'm very comfortable. I'm not wearing Nigerian dress—I'm not comfortable in Nigerian dress. That doesn't make me a non-Nigerian." This is the voice of choice, of the availability of styles, of mental as well as sensuous and material luxury. Perhaps it was purchased at great price. That is something I may discover while I'm here.

While I'm finding out about you, perhaps I should say a bit more about the literary situation of which I am part. I want to accompany this with what I should perhaps have started with, an apology for my ignorance of African history, culture, and languages. The apology is part of my situation, for until I made arrangements to come here a few months ago, I knew even less about Africa than I do now. I had read a few African novels, had once met Emphahlele and had heard Achebe lecture, but my larger picture of Africa was composed of simplicities derived from early readings of Conrad, Hemingway, Joyce Cary, Isak Dinesen, and Graham Greene. These infiltrated old images from movies and children's books.

In view of the fact that half my fellow Chicagoans trace their ancestry to this continent, my ignorance is particularly shameful, though it is one I share with even those on whose faces Africa is inscribed. Modern urban life has encapsulated too many of its memories in museums and libraries. Until recently—let's say the last quarter of a century—there was not only no attempt made to make one's ancestral past a part of one's life, there was a conscious effort to ignore, if not to hide it. American life seemed almost as history-less as the Rome of Augustus. I live in a city one of whose glories was the preservation of restaurants, costumes, songs, and stories of many different groups, Polish, Greek, Lithuanian, Swedish, Chinese, Irish, Jewish, and black. These neighborhoods have almost disappeared and only Chicago's urban politics—which appeals for votes to such groups—takes account of them. In addition, the varieties of American speech were getting homogenized out of existence by the dominant, flat voice of radio and early television. What was best preserved of the local was often found in novels and stories.

From the middle of the nineteenth century, the finest American writers have spoken with assignable accents. (And I include Henry James, who may be said to speak the convoluted, qualified speech of the parish of Intellect.) I know too little African literature to distinguish a local note in the English fiction of, say, Chinua Achebe and Ayi Kwei Armah or in the French of Mongo Beti, Birago Diop, Sembène Ousmane, or Cheikh Hamidou Kane, but my guess is that the distinctions will not lie so much in their sentence structure and rhythms, but in their subjects and their attitudes toward them. My view differs from that of Jean-Paul Sartre. In my only meeting with him he said he thought that the true *avant-garde* would be in Africa, where the speech of the colonizer would be transfigured by the voice and thought of the colonized. French intellectuals of this century, themselves sometimes the sons and grandsons of colonizers, have been perhaps too self-congratulatory about the opportunities their colonizing ancestors bestowed upon the colonized. André Gide said it was *"parmi les produits de croisement . . . des exigences opposées, que se recrutent les arbitres et les artistes,"* and even someone as ignorant as I knows that for many years, the theme of *exigences opposées,* the human being caught between cultures in what Cheikh Hamidou called *L'aventure ambiguë,* became an axiom of African thought. Perhaps this is a way in which the African situation is comparable to the American one.

For two hundred fifty years English literature has been compounded of both a central English assertion and an Anglo-Irish counter-assertion. From the time of Swift through that of Wilde, Shaw, Yeats, Joyce, Synge, and Beckett, it can be said that the *avant-garde,* the mockers, the parodists, the insiders-posing-as-outsiders have been Irish. From the middle of the nineteenth century, they were also Americans. In America itself the inside-outsiders have been stamped with locality: there were first the new English of New England, Thoreau, Emerson, and Hawthorne, and then the three great New Yorkers, Melville, Whitman, and James. These outsiders were less and less close to the inside. In the post-World War I period, the Southerners, the grandsons of defeated soldiers, began their literary invasion of the heartland. Faulkner, the agrarian poets of Nashville, Katherine Anne Porter, Eudora Welty, Flannery O'Connor, and many others including such fine new writers as Barry Hannah have carried the comedy of dissent into the textbooks of America. After World War II, the Jewish-American writers, assimilating the immigrant speech of fathers and grandfathers, mounted the next assault on the interior. Saul Bellow, J. D. Salinger, Norman Mailer, Philip and Henry Roth, Grace Paley, Bernard Malamud, Mark Harris, and many others have created the mental picaresques of new urban comedy. (Just coming to the threshold of important literature are the black writers, following the pioneer work of Richard Wright, Ralph Ellison, and James Baldwin.) All these inside-outsiders speak with the special music of their own brand of American. The beauty of their work is in no small part their idiomatic variations of English. This is more important than any technical or structural novelty, and it is a new turn in twentieth-century modernity. Joyce discovered that the modern style was the abandonment of personal style; American postwar writing is a return to it. It is also a return to the novel of character, for, after all, what would a disembodied voice mean? Nothing. The voice must come from an individual. So back into the middle comes the novel of character, character described or expressed as minutely as it's ever been in literature.

The central characters are, as you can imagine, almost always rebels, outsiders. After all, the modern writer is almost always an outsider himself. What makes a man or woman a writer in cultures which center around food and fuel, banking and government? It must be at least a small act of rebellion, a small disgust with material life, a need to dream, a desire to create one's own system. To some degree, every modern writer is like Kafka's Hunger Artist, who became an artist of fasting because he never found anything he liked to eat. The governors and bankers of the world have tried to slip the artist into the circus.

(Better this, perhaps, than the Church.) The artist, though, knows the governor's secret. He knows that society requires more than a touch of the poet, knows that human society cannot revolve about the dollar, the copper mine, and the lump of coal, that the soul requires more than computer systems, service stations, grocery stores, and can openers. Somewhere, somehow, the statues and the books contain, like tribal totems, the meaning as well as the glory of the human enterprise. This is the residue of the centuries of religious thought. So the outsiders, the writers, their narrative dreams painted in the local colors of a language which is itself a secret history of human activity, continue to play an essential part in the formation and continuity of the culture. I'm sure I will find that is the way it is here [in Rabat, Freetown, Lomé, etc.] as well.

# EXCERPTS FROM A REPORT

A few words about Africa from this non-Africanist:

1. Morocco. The universities were on strike, although I did lecture to a group at the new (indeed abuilding) Caid y Ali University in Marrakech. The strike centered on the limitation on government fellowships, which meant a narrowing of job opportunities for graduates. All through Africa, the traditional aggressive restlessness of students constituted a major problem for governments. So the University of Benin (in Cotonou) was closed (supposedly because the government was unable to pay salaries; it opened shortly after I left) and in Kenya, the government had extended the Easter vacation (forward!) because of complaints about the size of fellowships. After talking with Moroccan intellectuals and students as well as with some of the splendid young women attached to the International Cultural Agency, I'd like to venture a guess that the winds of change in the Arab world—at least here in Morocco—will come from neither traditionalists repelled by modernization nor from the ideologists (left or right), but from the women's movement.* One young woman told me, "In ten years, Moroccan women will run the country." That would seem to me more battle cry than sensible prediction, but one sensed here energy, purpose,

---

*After reading Jane Condon's *A Half-Step Behind* (Dodd, Mead, 1985), I'd say the same winds are blowing in Japan. As for the U.S.A., I know enough to know I don't know enough to guess what winds are blowing here.

74

intelligence, and a sophisticated awareness of the world. This despite official sensitivity to the written word. (No one is questioned more closely at the borders than a writer. "Writer of what?" one's asked—angrily.) There are too many soldiers around, but of course Morocco is not only fighting a war, it is a redoubt in a region made tipsy by the well-heeled revolutionary dreamer Qaddafi. The intellectual tension represented by the writers' linguistic and cultural conundrums (Arabic/French/Berber, Western/Moroccan) is spelled out in a country of vivid contrasts—biblical stretches of desert, date palms, shepherds, Arab markets, storytellers, snake charmers and the Western excitements of rock, action movies, video cassettes and Western luxe.

2. Sierra Leone. This is Africa. The airport's cut out of jungle, the road to the ferry is lined with shacks (as well as airplane billboards), and lines of African women (hip instead of breast-centered) head-carrying their fruit and jugs to Freetown. The magnificent colors of African dress, the ease of flesh, the suckling babies, the mutual grooming, the long patience, and then the ugly decrepitude of Freetown with its fringe of tourist magnificence (and ocean homes for the Lebanese merchants and other masters of the small economy). The famous old university, Fourah Bay, on the hill, with the elevator that hasn't functioned in three years and the bookstore with its few hundred volumes scarcely read (I found two copies of a book of mine that had been out of print ten years). The tin shacks, the waterless, lightless rooms where decent people live, the dirty streams where people urinate and wash clothes, the flaking, creaky sadness of Victorian brick. Graham Greene made a cult of the seediness (and the City Hotel bar is a memorial to his sad amusement). Mistakes: Japanese ferries unused because of the harbor's shallowness (up for sale); the Russians trawling up the fish (the contract expires in '82); the Chinese-built stadium which seems too grand for the most sports-hungry country. The old president manages the tensions (tribal resentment of the Freetown Krios—descendants of slaves freed by England during our revolution). Still, enormous sweetness and charm

as people somehow manage. Yet poverty grinds, and shame and fury will be held down only so long.

3. Togo. Here one sniffed ambition and hope. The heavy-jawed boss, his military strut exhibited—by North Korean sculptors—in all town squares and hotels, is part of a system which will not risk free thought. (Even in Freetown, there was an opposition sheet, its four orange, malprinted pages full of scandals which were then taken up by the official press. The president had just had a second-in-command arrested for defalcation.) In Freetown, the intelligentsia either work for the government or live in France. They handle information or teach medieval literature (the son of the Speaker of the House told me Rabelais is very African in his scatological religiosity and robust libertinage). Here I encountered the great sweetness and hunger for learning (though that was also in Freetown), and I went up country to the École Normale in Atakpame as well as Lomé. The world is very big beyond little Togo and the Togolese young want some of it. (They are proud of having been a German *Meisterkolonie* and of traveling as experts to other African countries.)

4. Benin. Here is real poverty, dust, the smallest variety of goods, a system that lives in part off smuggling (such things as whiskey) to Nigeria. The tininess of enterprise—a few wire cables here, a bunch of screws there, a case of Jack Daniels(!) for the equivalent of three dollars a fifth next to it—and the heaviness of a government modeled after the inappropriate Soviet one makes for tragicomedy. Fetish all around (I observed python-gods in Ouidah). I spoke with a marvelous old sculptor and home zookeeper (a boa, a few monkeys and birds) who cast my fortune with fetish bones. With marvelous charm and energy he waits for something to open up, visitors, news. As does Mr. Morgan, who runs a terrific little three-table restaurant and who's wandered over West Africa to settle in Cotonou. So people who would be brilliant and prominent achievers in other societies make do in their tiny homes. Unemployment, begging, sadness, these hang over this little country. My second lecture drew some intellectuals out of the woodwork (including the official wood-

work) and lo and behold they were hungrier than anyone for talk of high destiny, individuality, and self-expression.

5. Gabon. The great success story, with oil (and President Albert Bongo turning into El Hajj Omar Bongo) and much sophistication out of France. I appeared on television with the charming young daughter of the Vice-Premier back from France to write the first Gabonais novel, *Elonga*, about fetishism and its reach into every home, high and low. (She charmingly believes in it herself and argues with a forceful young woman judge about its importance. The French penal code had defined and condemned it, and the judge—herself marked by tribal cuts—spelled out the complexities of condemning a man who killed when he felt he'd been bewitched.) Libreville is luxurious and full of French. Still, there's the great African market and the tiny, filthy towns. (I went on the last of the travelable road to the outpost of M'bigou where a few wretched people cut and sell the sculpture that's Gabon's most famous artistic export.) Beyond, in the jungle, they're beginning to make mineral surveys. Only six or seven hundred thousand people, a well-run and benevolently dominated government (conforming to the IMF plans laid down four years ago), a haven for the Guineans who fled their miserable dictatorship (overthrown a year or so ago), and Cameroonians finding employment here. (Little is sadder or more fascinating than the beggars of Douala.) There's also a new tourist industry promoted by articles in French travel magazines. The European radio program Europe-1 has sent announcers and technicians to start up Africa-1, and it now broadcasts Africa-wide its sophisticated reports on the world. There is money here, and it will spread, but I saw nothing of the interior. (I heard a bit about it from such people as our able ambassador. He spoke of the rebuilding of Lambaréné in accord with Schweitzer's ideas of natural "air-conditioning.") The level of sophistication here among students (as well as ministers) is higher than in Benin or even Togo.

6. Zambia. Another benevolently led country, but one trapped by copper prices and veiling its economic problems with rhetoric about South Africa and Western threats. Still, this is as lively a

place intellectually as I found in Africa. Underneath the carapace of soldiers, there is great hunger to join the large world—but in the African way. The word has power here in Zambia. There is a loyal—and exceptional—group of whites (there's a wonderful dean of education at the university, Dr. Coombe), and there are excellent relations between Western and local cultural groups. I think Zambians feel that they're a crucible of the African future. (Its shape is a rough miniature of the heart-shaped continent.) Its experienced president is one of the original leaders of independence. There is good debate in the newspaper, and the university is lively. What's needed is an agricultural miracle or two and something besides copper.

7. Kenya. I can say even less here. Its magnificence is well known. Its drought-oppressed agriculture is troubled, though the Rift Valley and the coffee and tea plantations are beautiful and flourishing. Tea and coffee prices oppress. The cultural bureaucracy is heavy, but Kenyan ingenuity skirts the polite heavyweights. (I speak from the small experience of doing a radio program.) There is a large appeal by writers to those who speak their own language; the few writers with whom I spoke worked in two and sometimes three languages (in order to give pleasure to their own group as well as to reach larger audiences). There are lots of bidonvilles (the "estates") which suffer the usual miseries plus water shortages. Each one seems to have a hall where television is watched. (Over Africa reigns *The Incredible Hulk*—who embodies the power of rage.) Gujarati merchants run the tours and tailor shops. The university has a fine plant. The tourist industry flourishes (even the elephants and lions adjust to photographing incursions). Kenya looks as if it can absorb everything, but its beauty makes one yearn for the Africa that was already passing in Isak Dinesen and Elspeth Huxley's time.

8. All of Africa sweetens and breaks your heart, but Rwanda does it most of all. The smallest country and as poor or poorer than Benin. Five million people cultivating as many inches of the hills as they can. The main highway's only half-built, and trucks and cars flounder like whales in the muck. The cities are

tiny, but charming. The intellectual capital is Butare (though the government is going to split the small university in two to have a northern center as well), and the young people who run it and the students who fill it are as interesting as any I met. They are hungry for and read books more than anybody (though everywhere this need is enormous). They are landlocked, there are fewer opportunities to leave. (Who cares about little Rwanda? No joke this.) Yet they have the advantage of one national language, the complex and rich Kinyawanda (if I spell it right), and this is spoken by another five or six million outside the country. They thus have the makings of a small nation, and their boundaries are not the idle invention of Berlin conferenciers, but integral. I had the outstanding experience of my trip here. A commune staged a dance for me, and it was what Richard Wagner thought he could produce by himself, a *Gesamtkunstwerk*, a total work of art that embraced poetry, music, dance, costume, and theater. It was magnificent and the people's reaction to my enormous gratitude unfolded in the beautiful innocence of human flowers. My heart stays in little Rwanda, and I hope our government helps it, even though it is apparently without strategic interest. There is one potential worm in its apple, and that is the old conflict of Hutu and Tutsi, though the government plays this down and many don't actually know who is what, but a Tutsi to whom I talked said that he could never be sure when the policy would change and he'd lose his job to a Hutu.


2

In my opinion, much of the world's future will be determined in this continent. What we have in these twenty-year-old countries is the sort of spirit which you find in the debates and literature of eighteenth-century America. There is a combination of sophistication (derived from colonial training) and innovative (and often innocent) energy rising from the pragmatic encounters of nation-building. The difficulties are immense: tribal complexity, linguistic diversity, undeveloped agriculture, an enormous distance to go in training sophisticated technicians and civil servants, a confusion of ideologies, and limitations on free expression. But there are also enormous resources, the *least* of which are the old organic and inorganic compounds which still build and fuel the world. The most important resource is just that variety of person which is now a political handicap. The United States is what it is because of the variety of its citizens (the ways of thought, language, and custom, perhaps even physiology and immune systems). In one African country after another, you see and hear the benefits of exchange and interchange. The sophistication which knowledge of different languages involves does not stop with speech. It promotes openness, it creates absorptive power, it sharpens the eye for diversity, it creates pools of option. I heard and participated in many lively debates in Africa. These are no more fruitless palaverings than were the debates of the Virginia House of Burgesses.

Then there is the vastness and variety of the continent, the grandeur of rivers, desert, and mountain. One needn't be a poet to realize the stimulus to dream and accomplishment landscape gives. It offers images of aspiration and surmountable obstacle, it constitutes frontier, and no sophisticated American is unaware how important *frontier* is to a developing society.

A word too about what I will risk calling the African temperament. Obviously, there is an enormous variety of character, personality, and temperament on this vast continent, but it may be clearer to a transient than an old hand that there is a temper different from that of the majority of people elsewhere. The temperament is deeply good-natured, deeply informed by the two African seasons, the long and sunny benevolence and the shorter, powerful rainy one. No group in my experience seems to exist more in tune with the givens of nature, and though this can be an exasperation to someone like myself who lives less by sun and season than by watch and schedule, I see it now as an advantage and eventual power. There is much hatred slumbering under African geniality (I could spot that in the—usually—awful stories and poems of young people which I was given), but essentially there is less hatred, more ease of mind, less propensity to terror, perversion, and psychosis than I've seen elsewhere.

80

Yet many people live in ways which would drive most people I know out of their minds.

My own mission—and I began to conceive of it this way before long—was to let Africans know the function of a writer in a developed society. I tried to suggest that writers—people who were generalists except when they acted as guardians, purifiers, and enrichers of the language, people who extended the range of experience and who introduced different models of behavior while they were deepening and lightening the lives of their readers—were crucial to their own societies as well. Writers have been among the least welcome of the professionals in most of these countries. As they represented a threat in Plato's ideal order, so they suggest instability and disorder to the ruling classes here. I met only one writer who supported himself as a writer. (He is a Kenyan who writes and publishes his own potboilers.) Most of the francophone writers live in France. The writers who stay work in ministries. It is that or writing for no money and the threat of prison. Eastern Europe is by no means the only literary inferno on earth.

# WHEELS, SALMON, AND THE JARGON OF JACKDAWS

*I wasn't cut out for this life, see. I found myself in it. Like a wheel, it goes back and forth, what can it do . . . . yet something bitter stays inside me.*
—*from* Senza patente *by Gavina C.* Una prostituta racconta il mondo

*THE COOK: I couldn't buy the salmon.*
*SORBONNE DOCTOR: Why not?*
*C: An alderman was haggling over it.*
*SD: Here are a hundred écus. Buy me the salmon and the alderman.*
—*Chamfort,* Petits dialogues philosophiques

*. . . often did ravens croak*
*as they divided among themselves the cadavers*
*while jackdaws announced in their own jargon*
*that they were about to fly to the feed.*
—The Song of Igor's Campaign. *Translated from Old Russian by Vladimir Nabokov*

*This section deals with making public sense and public nonsense out of turmoil and violence. It also takes up the largely haphazard poetry which rises from the street. It includes scenes from an unpublished and unproduced play which, it seems to the un-lucky—unskillful?—playwright, bears on these issues. It also in-cludes two poems with an explanation of their presence. (The poet has been knocking uselessly at the Muse's door for most of his life.)*

# STREET POETRY AND A FALL FROM GRACE

Throughout most of history, the ordinary man has been heard only through the genial re-creation of extraordinary men. Our notion of saloon keepers and thieves, pimps, sailors, hangmen, and barbers comes to us by way of *The Canterbury Tales, The Satyricon, Celestina,* the poetry of Villon and Lorenzo de Medici ("La nencia da barberino"), the prose of Dekker, Greene, Quevedo, La Sage, and Defoe. Until our own time, the literate have learned next to nothing of ordinary men in their own words. Jest books, rogue and cony-catching pamphlets, trial records, parliamentary reports, dictionaries of "flash" and cant language, a few autobiographies by people who've transcended their origins, and some fragments supplied by such brilliant Boswells of the pavement as George Borrow and Henry Mayhew give us rougher cuts of ordinary lives, but it is really only our time of portable recorders that has begun to harvest the poetry of nonwriters.

One of the great products of democratic culture may be that millions of people who would have been called "undistinguished" now believe they are worth the distinction of being heard and recorded. No longer are the lives of saints, sages, poets, heroes, and kings the only ones inflected with destiny. Now almost anyone within reach of an inquiring reporter can believe that even his sense of failure is of public significance. We've become a nation of Rousseaus, and are ready to reveal to recorder and camera details that the frankest of autobiographers would have hidden in the ages of discreet heroism.

85

It is this affluence of self-confidence that makes possible books about the semi-literate assembled by people who, a century ago, would not have called themselves writers. Macaulay thought the case of Boswell unique, a man who wrote a book without having any literary gifts, a man whose very weakness—"officiousness . . . effrontery . . . toad-eating . . . the insensibility to all reproof"—enabled him to write the greatest of biographies. Today, some of the most fascinating books in existence are produced by people who don't have a tenth of Boswell's literary gift.

I suppose the forerunner of the modern tape-recorder book is *The Children of Sanchez*. Oscar Lewis spent thousands of hours recording the Sanchez family, then pruned, spliced, and ordered the results into a documentary saga; that is, a book with significant development and powerful resolution. A few years later, Studs Terkel, drawing on years of sympathetic radio interviews, worked out a more open, panoramic container for his Chicago portraits of *Division Street: America*. Since then, he's assembled books on such topics as the Depression and Working. Auden wrote that asking the hard question was easy, but not everyone can ask so many; and few of us have the patience and charm to draw such a variety of good stories as a good interviewer.

Other "authors" use such principles of inclusion as "A Day in the Life of . . . " or "What I Was Doing When X Happened." There are endless frame-stories, some looser than that of *The Canterbury Tales*, some defined narrowly and strictly.

Ira Berkow's book *Maxwell Street* (1977) describes the famous flea market and immigrant ghetto whose chief artery is a mile-long street a mile south of the Loop. Today, Maxwell Street is a few blocks of boarded tenements and brick dust and a few blocks of raucous market. Berkow's fifty interviews with Maxwell Streeters are arranged chronologically and spliced with commentary and newspaper entries which spell out the street's decline for most of its eighty-odd years. Today it's more black and gypsy than Jewish; the recent inhabitants have not had the chance to become famous. What counts for Berkow—and the reader—though is that its rough commerce still nourishes vivid speech: the flamboyance of the hard sell, the rhythm, incisiveness, and color of self-defense and self-justification, the brio of the tough and those who defend themselves against the tough.

Again and again the boast is, "If you can survive on Maxwell Street, you can survive anywhere." Out of this world of fist and con have come an amazing number of the famous (or their parents)—Paley of CBS, Balaban of Paramount, Elaine May and Benny Goodman, Meyer Levin and Arthur Goldberg, Hyman Rickover and Col. Jake Arvey, Barney Ross, Jack Ruby and "Greasy Thumb" Guzik. Great Chicago and national fortunes began in the covered stalls and the piles of damaged yard goods and stolen watches. Berkow's tape recorder registers the celebrities (or their relatives) and with them salesmen, hustlers, doctors, delicatessen owners, judges, policemen, Jews, blacks, gypsies, Italians. The book is a grand portrait gallery, and in its way a historical treasury, for every man is an annal, and there are details here about the recognition of Israel and the actions of such non-Maxwell Street celebrities as Jack Johnson and Ronald Reagan* that will be incorporated in appropriate histories. There are as well pocket manuals of the hard-sell and terrific picaresque stories and scenes.

In short, a fetching book, even though its author-assembler is stranded in the wastes of the language and loses battle after battle to that toughest of heavyweights, the English sentence.

2

If Lewis, Terkel, Berkow, and others record the street poetry of amateurs, there are other amateurs who fail because they seem too professional for the occasion. James Watt, Ronald Reagan's first secretary of the interior, lost his post because of his excellent poet's ear. He fell from political grace because of meter. A century earlier, James Blaine lost an election because of his gift for

---

*Major Sidney Bartlett, an Air Force bombardier in World War II, was furious after reading an article called "Ronald Reagan Goes to War" for "I knew what that meant . . . driving five miles up Ventura Boulevard" to order underwear for the troops. He approached Reagan after a speech in which he recommended that we go to war with Russia and asked, "Does that mean you go too?"

alliteration. (He called the opposition the party of "rum, Romanism and rebellion.") Actually, the root of Mr. Watt's trouble is perception, not style, but the style of his utterance made it memorable, i.e., devastating. "A black, a woman, two Jews and a cripple," said Mr. Watt of a committee he'd chosen. A grand toothy smile spread over his lunar face. Why not? He'd come up with a flawless Shakespearean line, three iambs, a pyrrhic and a trochee—or anapest—in the eleven syllables. No poet could be expected to impair such a line by substituting "handicapped person" for "cripple" or "professor of political science" for "Jew."

Pascal said a person shouldn't be indicted for saying what others had said. After all, in a tennis match, both players used the same ball. The winner was the one who placed it best. Secretary Watt was the literary McEnroe of the administration, a placement artist whose previous triumph was "Let Reagan be Reagan."

History, as a form of organized memory, is full of memorable speech. "If this be treason, make the most of it" is an even more perfect pentameter line than Watt's.

Unfortunately for politician poets, many voters feel uncomfortable in the poetic grip and use such words as "spellbinder" and "demagogue" to loosen it. Ranke wrote that Macaulay's style prevented him from telling the truth, meaning that Macaulay's words were chosen for rhythm as much as accuracy. *Nicht gut*, thought Ranke. There is—let us try our poetic hand— a hint of mendacity in music.

Mr. Watt's ex-Boss understands public utterance as well as anyone around. (It may be said that this is most of what he understands.*) He has a good feel for the rhythm and dynamics of expression. He certainly understands rhetorical overkill. Mr.

---

*March, 1986. In the interest of fairness, let me say that a distinguished economist who knows and works with the president just told me that he is better informed about economics than any of the three or four presidents with whom he's worked. He attributes this to the reading Mr. Reagan did between jobs (Hayak, von Mises) and the soundness of the elementary text he used as an economics major at Eureka College.

Watt's poetry was once an administrative plus: its excess could be publicly rebuked, and the rebuker made to look good by contrast. The Rebuker, Reagan, is also a horseman (species, Hollywood and Vine). Secretary Watt pulled too hard on the poetic bit and the Horseman reluctantly retired him to pasture.

The moral here is that the idiosyncratic poetry of the street gratifies us because it makes remarkable those who haven't been remarked. As for the rhetorical poetry of our bosses, we Americans don't like it. It smells of the Phony. Boss-poetry must be offhand, folklike, not mandarin. It must look surprised at itself.

# LANGUAGE AND TURMOIL

A century or two ago, back in 1968, the melting pot melted away. In the Bay Area it had been overheating for years; and for four years, it had been hottest on the Berkeley campus. In 1968, the action crossed the bay to the "instant campus" of the streetcar college a mile from the Pacific, San Francisco State. The Black Student Union there was pulling the place together like a fist. Hatred, organized by pick-me-ups from Marx, Mao, Fanon, and Cleaver, ignited that ever-ready resentment of the sympathetic young for whatever seems an obstacle to fairness and the pursuit of joy.

The process was from complaint to confrontation, raids to riots. The slack-jawed appetite of news-consumers brought cameras and reporters which simplified, distorted, and created that instant stage which made all but the purest and most naive self-conscious actors. The expert rousers of California lined up as antagonists, the imagery of the state's most famous industry shaping the rhetoric. Eldridge Cleaver, a candidate for president of the United States, worked over a crowd of six thousand students and faculty. He analyzed the ghetto word "m.....f....." (sic) and applied it precisely to his presidential rivals. The obscenity went against professorial grain. Language defined the

Leo Litwak and Herbert Wilner, *College Days in Earthquake Country: A Personal Record.* New York: Random House, 1971.

expertise of the university. "We were one community only because language made it so," writes the novelist-professor Leo Litwak. "Cleaver tried to unmake it." Cleaver took aim at the old movie star who was the state's governor. "One knew that movies were into a make-believe bag, but the unreality espoused on the screen by the flat souls of such pablum-fed actors as Reagan reflected to me—black ghetto nigger me—a sickening mixed bag of humorless laughter and perfect Colgate teeth, with never a real hint of the funk of life." This blurred poetry washed out the lines between words, images, make-believe and what seemed the real thing on this word-locked green, deeds, movement, blood, structural change. For the misappraised or mistreated, this was more than hope; it was the vertiginous excitement of *the reality fix*.

For another group, made up largely of sensitive, sedentary men, content after long climbs into burgher security but discontented with their failure to feel in their own experience the passions and meaning of what they taught, the battle call wasn't so simple. Litwak, for instance, was the son of a Detroit union man; he had met Jimmy Hoffa and been impressed by his verve and toughness; he knew what a union meant. He'd also talked at length with Reagan and seen him as more than a sleek doll. Reagan was naive but alert, persuasive, combative. His movie career had sunk in. "After a series of reluctant performances as . . . Shirley Temple's first screen lover and Bozo the Chimp's attendant, Reagan finally became a cowboy. The role swallowed him. Inside the semblance of a hawk-eyed gunfighter was a nearsighted man who wore contact lenses. Inside the semblance of a warrior was a man who spent the years as a Special Services officer in Hollywood." Uncomfortable with the simplicities of both the Cleaver and the Reagan world, Litwak worked out his stand and joined the new professor's union.

So did his colleague, Herbert Wilner. Wilner had grown up in Brooklyn slums. He'd worked his way out and up through books and athletics. A fine teacher and story-writer, a responsible, honorable man, Wilner had spoken up early against the violence and then had felt the awful pain behind it. It was necessary for him to take a special stand. He too had larger views of both sides. Reagan had found his deputy in a trim little Japanese-American semanticist named Hayakawa. Wilner had driven home from a party with the man and remembered his resentment against the "great universities [which] had no appreciation of his work. Harvard and Chicago were named particularly and often. A man as well known in his work as he might have expected a chair . . . but the rigidities and snobberies of tradition stood in his way." So in classic fashion, the insulted and injured were faced by a recruit risen from their ranks. Tough, sportive, buoyed by publicity, Hayakawa triumphed. Wilner, who could have eased himself behind the authority of police and the state's Reagan-fed resentment, also went into the professors' union.

Day after day, these necktied men filed between the truncheons of police and the screaming students. Demands, speeches, strikes, bones cracked, flesh bloodied. And then the energy, money, and excitement drained away. It was over. Everyone more or less lost. And won. Student leaders went briefly to jail, then turned towards pacifism, yoga, law school. Hayakawa became a hero/villain, Litwak and Wilner sat down to think and work on their fine book.

If these days now seem more remote than the Gallic Wars, Litwak and Wilner, thoughtful scribes and decent warriors, are part of a present that will stay present.

*The poems which follow were written during the Time of Trouble at the University of Chicago in 1971. The focus of the trouble was a young woman professor who'd been denied tenure in the Department of Sociology. Spurred by clever organizers— a few of whom are still being hunted by the FBI—a couple of hundred students, asweat with revolutionary and sexual excitement, occupied—one of the key verbs of modern political "turmoil"—the Administration Building. There were meetings, day and night, speeches, slogans, theater in the streets, and many declarations about the meaning and purpose of universities. Poems were my public contribution to the excitement. The first one—*

*omitted here because it's choked with local reference—was a mock-heroic obscenity of fifty or sixty lines which appeared in the campus paper (the crucial medium of information and inflammation). It was said to have helped convert the cauldron into a comedy. The others were written in different meters, for it occurred to me that the progress of events was a microcosm of European events which had been poetically expressed in different meters. So the first poem printed here adapted Giuseppi Giusti's famous revolutionary poem "The Steam-driven Guillotine"; the second was bent into the meters of Wordsworth's great ode.*

### On a Hint from Signor Giusti

In the heart of China
They've found a steam machine,
infinitely finer
than a guillotine.
A thousand heads an hour
      feel its power.

It's caused an uproar here.
Deans realize
That, front to rear,
We could civilize;
And rear to front,
      Confront.

Prexy's an honest man,
a little stingy, a bit of a brute,
not brilliant, but then,
he loves Verdi and the flute,
and protects
      intellects.

Bach-haired kids
Gripe and disrupt.
Jigs and yids
Corrupt.

## The Position of the Body

Now here's a tool
To keep heads cool.

Our Chaplain said, "Let's baptise
the sweet machine."
"Why not," said our man-size
Dean.
"When such genius springs
          Under our wings."

## Song from a Sit-In
(February, 1969)

There was a time when campus, lab and class
      Did seem to me
Expressions of a beauteous law.
      Now I turn
      Here where I learn
And what was once so fair seems to me fair no more.

      The great speak out
      Of antique rout;
    The books emit their love
    Within the empery of mind;
    The Gothic walls above
      Embrace their kind,
And yet I feel a motion in this place
      That chills its grace.

School is its own joy and measure, yes,
      But yet I feel,
    Moving from class to class,
    That I am seen and see
    Within a shaded glass,
      That my own weal
      But serves to show
    The brutalized and slow
That they are that because of me.

# Wheels, Salmon, and the Jargon of Jackdaws

This, my instructors dear,
You may not guess,
Examining your difficult books and maps,
But it is, nonetheless,
What boils my own fear
And brings me close to those
Who see a rose
Within collapse.

I know that you perhaps see only loss.
At times I too
Detest this force.
But how be true?
It is not in my power to be you,
Hardly to be me.

Looking last night at the moon
It seemed much closer to me
Than it did two months ago.*
Is it too soon
To know
If the gravity of my act
Binds you in fact
To me?

*A space ship had circled the moon at Christmas time.

# THE EMPEROR OF DICTIONARIES AND ITS
# SCIONS OF THE SEVENTIES

There is a story of Jorge Luis Borges about a remarkable crystal called El Aleph which contains every place and thing in the universe including itself.

I think of it because I have on this desk—though just barely—another Aleph, somewhat larger and somewhat more parochial, the two volumes which contain in miniature the thirteen volumes—fifty million words, 227,770,589 letters and figures—of that Emperor of Dictionaries, that Great Scion of the Gutenberg Family, the *Oxford English Dictionary.* In 1973 the first volume of the modern *Supplement* "recording the vocabulary of the Twentieth Century in all its complexity" was published.

"All its complexity?" Well, Alephants can exaggerate. Until this desk supports a screen fed by the Giant Computer of Every-Study-Logic-Language-and-History, these fantastic compendia will hold as much of what there is to know as anything that will ever sit on it.

The Great Dictionary began . . . Well, once upon a time (in 1842), a London Philological Society decided to revise the dictionary Samuel Johnson put together in 1755. Johnson's dictionary had been intended to fix the "mature" English language

---

*A Supplement to the Oxford English Dictionary,* edited by R. W. Burchfield. Vol. I, A–G. New York: Oxford University Press, 1973.
*The Compact Edition of the Oxford English Dictionary.* 2 Vol. Boxed with Bausch and Lomb magnifier. New York: Oxford University Press, 1971.

as the French Academy was fixing French and the Academia della Crusca was fixing Italian.

Johnson was too wise for this. In his marvelous Preface to the Dictionary, he wrote that the lexicographer who imagines "that the dictionary can embalm his language, and secure it from corruption and decay," was a derisive person: ". . . to enchain syllables, and to lash the wind, are equally the undertakings of pride, unwilling to measure its desires by its strength. . . ."

The wise Society decided to create a dictionary on historical principles. Each word would appear in its varied usages from its first to its most recent recorded appearances. Dated English writings would supply the evidence of usage.

The Society began its work in 1858. A biblical lifespan later, the *New English Dictionary* appeared, and five years after that, along with the American New Deal and the German New Order, appeared a *Supplement and Bibliography.* Thirteen volumes, 102 pounds, one yard's width of shelf space; a lexicographical Stonehenge.

In 1971, the Age of Miniaturization produced the Compact Edition. For $75, a good light, a strong table and a magnifying glass supplied in a slip drawer of the boxed volumes, a lover of words can settle in for a lustrum ("1601 Holland, PLINY 1.24. The Lustrum or computation of the five years beginneth at the leap yere, when the Dogstar doth arise") of verbal magellanizing (entry for the Supplement of 1997).

Some 16,400 pages reduced to 4,200, with every one of the 414,825 defined words micrographically present. May it replace the watch as the graduation present of the middle class.

The three-volume supplement will contain 50,000 main entries. Volume 1, A–G, contains almost 18,000 entries and 130,000 illustrative quotations. Newspapers and novels, poets and physicists, bankers and bookies (if they've talked for the record), whatever makes for modern writing in English is here.*

---

*I spent a good hour with Philip Roth checking out the obscenities marked by examples from *Portnoy's Complaint.* "I've made it for 'cunt,' but what about 'pussy'?"

Almost. For everybody will find the great dictionary lagging behind his own talk; and not just today's talk. So I found that the first entry for "Fatso" comes from a book on Duke Ellington published in 1944. I write here to witness—and confess—that I called Bobbie Reamer "Fatso" in 1940. (If this confession had appeared back then, perhaps a word-spotter would have found it and sent it along to Oxford so my nastiness would be emblazoned in the *Supplement*.)

As for the word "flaky," the good *Supplement* only records its connection with pastry. They've missed a lot of boats here.

As Johnson knew, there's no Aeolus for lexical wind. No academy can "guard the avenues of their languages . . . retain fugitives, and repulse intruders . . . sounds are too volatile and subtle for legal restraints. . . ."

The great Oxford Dictionary neither legislates nor incarcerates. It records, it defines, it illustrates. It is the cortex of our language, at least as much of it as lexical and editorial intelligence can supply. If Shakespeare is a Chartres Cathedral of English, these great dictionary-makers are the men who quarried his stones and then worshipped inside them.

# TIMERMAN AND NATIONAL MADNESS

*I write this as our first actor-president uses the vocabulary of
cop movies, rock music, and* Reader's Digest *patriotism to work
up the country against the—undoubtedly repressive—Sandinista
regime in Nicaragua. I believe more in the persistence of human
character than what are called historical forces. Otherwise, I
would see not just this president as a poor player upon a stage
enacting a script written by History.*

*In 1913, J. A. Hobson wrote of the*

> *familiar move in the high game of politics, by which the employing
> and possessing classes endeavour to divert the force of popular
> demands for drastic social reforms by thrusting to the front of the
> political stage one of the sensational issues of foreign policy kept
> for that purpose.*

> (The German Panic, *p. 29*)

*Hobson's notion was that surplus profits had to be invested abroad
so that, willy-nilly, an investor became an imperialist. A. J. P.
Taylor\* wrote that Hobson "did for Imperialism what Marx had
done for capitalism itself: he showed that it sprang from inevitable
economic causes, not from the wickedness of individuals." People
for whom the analysis of events largely consists of the condem-
nation or idolatry of individuals don't comprehend such notions.*

\**The Trouble Makers. Dissent Over Foreign Policy 1792–1939* (Bloomington:
Indiana University Press, 1958).

# The Position of the Body

*(For them, generality takes the form of conspiracy.) Novelists—*
*Tolstoy as well as Zola, Proust as well as Romains—work to show*
*individuals and the decisions they make created by rich contexts*
*(the positions of the body). Add up what goes into Pierre Be-*
*zukhov's head, and you may sum it up as either free will or*
*determinism. Tolstoy assigns free will to key moments, such as*
*the suspension of a fist from another's face. As for that Man of*
*Destiny, Napoleon, he's just that: a man—that is, a puppet—of*
*whatever forces, social, whimsical, eccentric, can be summed up*
*as destiny. Tolstoy sees Napoleon as I see Ronald Reagan, a man*
*dominated by his need to make an impression—in Reagan's case,*
*a genial impression—on other people. That he is generally de-*
*scribed, even by supposedly shrewd observers, as a "strong pres-*
*ident," inclines one to slide to the other end of the scale where*
*Marx, Hobson, and the Manchester Dissenters contrive their*
*generalizations. Here, at least, there is a tradition of witty crit-*
*icism. This, from John Bright's October, 1858, speech in Bir-*
*mingham, could, with a couple of changes, brighten the Op-Ed*
*page of tomorrow's* New York Times*:*

> *This foreign policy, this regard for the "liberties of Europe," this*
> *care at one time for "the Protestant interest," this excessive love*
> *for the "balance of power" is neither more nor less than a gigantic*
> *system of outdoor relief for the aristocracy of Great Britain.* (Great
> laughter.)

*In different ways, Timerman, Fussell, and Lewis belong to this*
*tradition of critical wit.*

Israel is desolated . . . Palestine has become a widow . . .
—"The Hymn of Victory over the Libyans," ca. 1220 B.C.
(The first recorded use of the name Israel.)

A nation gets something like a soul when it exists *for* something, when it ceases to exist solely as a gathering place for the
unwanted. It can also be said that a nation loses its soul when

---

Jacobo Timerman. *The Longest War. Israel in Lebanon*, trans. from Spanish
by Miguel Acoca. New York: Knopf, 1982.

its effort to preserve itself is deformed by natural paranoia or imperialistic ambition. "During Juan Peron's second and third presidential terms," writes Jacobo Timerman, "I saw Argentina seized by a collective madness." Then again, in 1977, Argentina was gripped by another seizure. Timerman, perhaps the country's most distinguished editor, publisher, and commentator, was seized and jailed. His account of this experience, *Prisoner without a Name, Cell without a Number,* was read around the world. He left Argentina—where his family had come from the Ukraine in 1928—and moved to Israel. There, in the summer of 1982, he again watched a country in the grip of hallucination and militarism. These—he writes in his journal of the terrible summer—were largely in the heads of two men, the obsessed and "unbalanced" old terrorist and lawyer, Menachem Begin, and the obese military genius, defense minister Ariel Sharon.

On June 6, Sharon launched the war which Israel knew he'd been wanting to fight for years. Called "Peace in Galilee," the Sharon offensive was supposed to clear forty kilometers of Lebanese territory to secure peace for Israel's northern border. No matter that the border had never been quieter or that three former chiefs of staff had declared that such a war could not secure anything (let alone solve the problem of the Palestinians). Sharon and Begin had at hand a great military instrument. When an Israeli diplomat was attacked in London, they took the opportunity to use it.

Israel had fought five wars of self-defense. Now it fought a war which troubled many of its citizens from the outset. Never before had serious debate about a war broken out as it was waged. Never before had the remarkable Israeli army been kept in the dark about its aims and objectives. Timerman reports an interview with soldiers: questioned about how far their army would advance, they joked, "Well, there's a vandalized synagogue in Ankara, so we will surely go there. Also there are Katyusha rockets in Moscow, so we will have to go take them out."

There was, says Timerman, a smell about this war. Soldiers and reporters spoke about a new "odor of death." The odor was that of the unburied bodies of children. The government's censorship couldn't screen out the smell. Nor could it screen out the pictures of destroyed cities, Tyre, Sidon, Damur. Menachem Begin's silver tongue glistened with the rhetoric of the Holocaust, but this time, Israelis made painful jokes about it. "He's getting his *shoa* [Hebrew for 'Holocaust'] on the road"; "We have no more blood left in our veins. Begin's spilled it all in his speeches."

Madness is contagious. The war opened sewers of anti-Semitism all over the world. Vicious talk of genocide and Hitler defaced the world's walls and privies. The PLO, ghostly apparatus of a ghost state, fed on the false promises of Arab and other countries, equipped with the antiquated surplus weaponry of the Eastern bloc, was ground down between Israeli tanks and the hypocritical rhetoric of its supposed supporters.

Something else happened. The Jews of the Diaspora found their tongue. No longer intimidated by Beginian criticism that they were self-hating anti-Semites, such men as Pierre Mendes-France, Nahum Goldmann, and Philip Klutznick called for "the reciprocal recognition of Israel and the Palestinian people." Jewish writers in Europe and America published appeals for clarity and reconciliation.*

In Israel, the man Timerman calls the finest and bravest officer in the army, Colonel Eli Geva, petitioned to be relieved of his command. He would fight alongside his men but not lead them against the children of Beirut. "Did you receive an order to kill those children?" asked his prime minister. "No? Then what are you complaining about." Colonel Geva was retired and the government boasted about "an army in which a colonel could make such a beautiful gesture."

In the Jerusalem *Post*, a letter was published.

I am the descendant of a rabbinical family, the only son of Simha Guterman, a Zionist and Socialist who died as a hero and a fighter against the Nazis in the Warsaw uprising. I was rescued from the Holocaust and brought to Israel. I served in the army and built

*The most moving to me was Primo Levi's piece in Rome's *La repubblica*.

102

my home in Israel. A son was born to me, called Raz—a son who grew up to be a great pride to his family, strong and beautiful and honest and upright in his character.

Raz Guterman was sent with his unit "in great haste and irresponsibility" to storm the Beaufort Castle where he died.

Before the blood was dry on the rocks of the mountain of Beaufort, Begin and Sharon hurried into their helicopters, surrounded by photographers.

Yaakov Guterman's letter ended,

May my great pain pursue them forever, the suffering of a father in Israel whose world has been destroyed and the joy of life destroyed in him forever.

On this bloody planet, fathers and mothers have suffered too much such pain. In the Israel of 1982, the pain was not tempered—as it had been in the past—by the sense of a just cause.

For some, no war is honorable, but for most of us, there are times when human haters with armies at their disposal must, one way or another, be stopped. For Yaakov Guterman and Jacobo Timerman, the horrible fact of 1982 was that the haters headed their own government.

Few wars turn nations inside out. When such wars occur, the war outside is part of the war within. (The French war in Algeria, and the American war in Vietnam, are two such wars.) Thucydides' account of the Peloponnesian War is the classic description of these wars of self-demolition.

Jacobo Timerman's book belongs more to the tradition of Jewish prophets than Greek classical historians. Its eloquence is not cool and sometimes overflows its subject. Yet Timerman, like Solzhenitsyn, speaks with the authority of the wounded. For those like me, in whom this war in Lebanon, like the one in Vietnam, festered (because of the special moral responsibility of the countries which waged it), Timerman's book brings the relief of passionate expression. It is also in part what it calls for, an attempt to repair the national soul which Ariel Sharon and Menachem Begin almost destroyed.

# THE DICTION OF WAR

> He's lost his color very far from here,
> Poured it down shell-holes till the veins ran dry,
> And half his lifetime lapsed in the hot race,
> And leap of purple spurted from his thigh.
> —Wilfred Owen, "Disabled"

England hadn't been in a major war for a century. Even in
the Boer War, there hadn't been machine guns or barbed wire
or trenches. War was gilded with the antique gallantries of Hen-
ty's boys' books, Tennyson's Arthurian poems, William Mor-
ris's medieval ones. Its vocabulary was as remote as the Round
Table: horses were *steeds*, the enemy was the *foe*, to attack was
to *assail*, to be earnestly brave was to be *gallant*, to be cheerfully
brave was to be *plucky*, actions were *deeds*, danger was *peril*, the
dead were the *fallen*, the chest was the *breast*, soldiers were
*warriors*, the blood of the wounded was "the red / Sweet wine
of youth" (Rupert Brooke). Paul Fussell—who made this list—
writes in his subtle account of the experience and literature of
the Great War of 1914–18, "This system of 'high' diction was
not the least" of the war's "ultimate casualties."

The root of Fussell's study is the transformation of experience
by the way it is recorded and thus, partially, felt. Minds are

---

Paul Fussell, *The Great War and Modern Memory.* New York: Oxford University Press, 1975.

prompted to receive certain messages. When the messages over-whelm the equipment of reception, new equipment must be made. The Great War overwhelmed the apparatus of receptivity. The instruments built to receive it are still in use. This is what Fussell demonstrates. The combat soldiers who "wrote the war" were not the greatest artists of the century, Proust, Joyce, Mann, Yeats, Lawrence, Musil, Rilke, or Kafka. These men felt the war deeply but indirectly. The men who recorded the war were Siegfried Sassoon, Robert Graves, Edmund Blunden, David Jones, Wilfred Owen, Isaac Rosenberg, and the authors of thou-sands of diaries and letters, many of which Fussell studied with that literary intelligence which can hear in the alteration of a traditional meter or the variation in a standard phrase a new mentality, an innovation in the imagination of experience.* Us-ing what may be more useful for him as an author than for us as readers, the distinctions Northrop Frye makes between mythic, plausible, and ironic fictions, Fussell describes the alterations in the attitudes, perception, and literature of English-speaking peo-ple from the publication of Hardy's "Satires of Circumstance" near the beginning of the war to the demonic war farces of Joseph Heller and Thomas Pynchon. En route, he touches on matters as small as the changes in pub times (the afternoon closing so the munition workers wouldn't stagger into the late shift) to such important ones as the insensitivity to atrocity stories which caused millions to disbelieve the actual atrocities of Hitler's Ger-many till millions more had paid terribly for the delay.

A powerful experience stuns the mind beyond discrimination, but memory demands filtration systems so that it can control not only what happened but what may come again. Many such systems are literary, and these direct the mind to certain portions

*In 1936, Ford Madox Ford described the effect of Stephen Crane's war novel on the unprepared generation: "Few had given any picture at all of post-Medieval warfare . . . and suddenly there was *The Red Badge of Courage*, showing us . . . how the normal, absolutely undistinguished, essentially ci-vilian man from the street had behaved in a terrible and prolonged war. . . ." "Stephen Crane," from *Portraits from Life* (New York: Houghton Mifflin, 1965), p. 22.

of a sensuous offering rather than others. They shape the way we see and the way we at least think we should feel about what happens. Fussell can show on the small scale how one literary tradition enabled English soldiers to see, or at least write about the scarlet poppies of Flanders, but ignore the equally widespread blue cornflowers. He also shows how a literary tradition of homoeroticism (an idealized homosexuality) dating from the Achilles/Patroclus section of *The Iliad* led enormous numbers of sensitive men to a heroism derived more from the defense of loved bodies near at hand than from the defense of home and country. A feeling for dawn, for sunset, for sky (the only thing glimpsed from the trenches), the terrible discrepancies between the mendacity of reportage and the smell, filth, stupidity, and murder of the front, the gulf between Staff (generals who hadn't seen a trench) and infantry, the sensitivity to the minute—a bird wing, a spur of light—these became the elements of a new apparatus of perception, the new code of war.

# THE ART OF WYNDHAM LEWIS

"Upward from the surface of existence a lurid and dramatic scum oozes and accumulates into the characters we see."

In his early novel, *Tarr,* Wyndham Lewis wrote that the statue's soul is its

> lines and masses. . . . No restless, quick flame-like ego is imagined for the inside of it. That is another condition of art; to have no inside, nothing you cannot see.

No ghost in these machines. Lewis's world was what is visible and what is done. He wrote about the art of ruling and the mechanism of action. Human beings were "apes of God."

Or so it seemed to him till things happened to as much as through him: illness, war, the scattering of friends, isolation. Then the ape of God became "an object of amazing interest," the painter's hand buried "Euclid deep in the living flesh," and Lewis painted the marvelous portraits of the late period, the famous Eliot now in South Africa and the dreaming Pound in London's Tate Gallery.

Then the second great war broke out, there were no more London commissions, and the old soldier of the First War emigrated to Canada, where he spent his time "self-condemned" in a Toronto hotel. Returning to England in 1946, he had another

---

Walter Michel, *Wyndham Lewis: Paintings and Drawings.* Berkeley: University of California Press, 1971.

# The Position of the Body

ten years to live, but only four to see. He painted another Eliot, hands on his old friend's face to compensate for dimming sight. Then he was totally blind. "Pushed into an unlighted room, the door banged and locked forever, I shall . . . have to light a lamp of aggressive voltage in my mind to keep at bay the night." The voltage finished his massive futurist novel, *The Human Age*.

Of men who've practiced two arts in this century—Lawrence, Cummings, Schoenberg, David Jones, Paul Klee—Lewis is the only one who pioneered in both. He had, said Eliot, "the thought of the modern and the energy of the cave man."

Walter Michel, the editor and assembler of an enormous book of Lewis's paintings and drawings, writes that Lewis began as a recruit in the Cézanne revolution. No Cubist, he "took from Cubism what he could use: 'the creative line, structure, imagination untrammelled by any pedantry of form or naturalistic taboo, a more vigorous shaping of the work undertaken.'" But Cubism, under the shadow of "the exquisite and accomplished, but discouraged, sentimental and inactive" Picasso, went "imitative and static."

In his periodical, *Blast*, Lewis announced a new art language, one that came from England, "that Siberia of the mind . . . the industrial (hence 20th century) country par excellence, whose 'steel trees where green ones were lacking' could offer to the painter 'wilder intricacies than those of nature.'"

The first war ended *Blast* and scattered the artists congregated in London (Gaudier, Epstein, Pound). But the foam of London was inflammable matter for Lewis's rage. He focused on Shakespeare's strangest hate-play, *Timon of Athens*, and did a portfolio of drawings, a fury of wedges, ellipses, askew boxes, black, white, gray, within which were fixed mangled arms, noses, black suns. And he painted *The Crowd*, an insoluble puzzle of lattices, gold frame lines, almost-figures, almost-structures seen in windows shut against no-outside. "Wars begin with this huge indefinite Interment in the cities," he wrote of "the crowd" in an unfinished novel.

The war "presented me with a subject-matter so consonant with the austerity of the 'abstract' vision I had developed that

108

it was an easy transition." (This from *Rude Assignment*, one of his two autobiographies.) He moved from battlefield sketches to paintings in which the war machine appears as a blast furnace whose parts and products are soldiers.

After the war, taking a harder grip on the natural, he did portraits. (They supported him.) In portraits, "a sort of immortality descends. . . . It is an immortality, which, in the case of the painting, the sitters have to pay for with death, or at least with its coldness and immobility."

With black chalk or pencil he placed in the centers of bare rectangles the precise, intense heads of Chesterton, Rebecca West, Noel Coward, Spender, Joyce, Eliot, McLuhan (a young enthusiast), Joseph Alsop (another young fan, who wrote an essay about him at Harvard and arranged a reading there).

The painter also wrote novels of granular precision and ironic fury, tracts, books on Shakespeare, on time, on power, on artists. As for his drawings and paintings, they are a treasury of shape, line, and sober intensities of color that will stand as his discovery, product and sign. The dust jacket of Michel's book carries what may be the most beautiful of all the portraits, the *Red Portrait* (1937), whose modest geometry and pervasive, green-lit reds flow into the living-room shapes (vase, books, mantel, lamp) and bloom in the luminous, calm facial planes of the artist's wife.

# NADIA AND THE ALBATROSS

*Ce voyageur ailé, comme il est gauche et veule!*

  At twenty-one, Baudelaire wrote a poem about a great albatross flying regally in the air until, pulled down by sailors, it staggered foolishly around the deck. This poet's image of the poet came to mind when I read Aleksandr Solzhenitsyn's speech at the 1978 Harvard commencement. For its speaker, the senior class had invited Woody Allen, a hawk who pretends to be an albatross. When he declined, they settled for a self-parodying chicken, Rodney Dangerfield. To match so celebrated a speaker, the adult contingent invited Solzhenitsyn. He came down from the green hills of Vermont—his last such descent—and delivered himself of an hour-long jeremiad about those who had invited him, their relatives, friends, and ideological siblings everywhere. The West, said the Great Exile—speaking to its creamy representatives—was a spineless, pleasure-drunk collection of legalistic hair-splitters. It was conformist and fashion-crazed, a technocratic excrescence of that secular humanism which rose in the Renaissance and sped tragically into Marxism. Westerners were totally unfit for their great task: "the ultimate conflict with Evil." They would lose that conflict and be turned into a Cambodian ant colony. (The Russian albatross saw no reason to felicitate the graduates.)

  Some of the audience, like the sailors in Baudelaire's poem, were amused by the speech. Kings used to hire fools, and com-

110

fortable people still pay well to hear themselves denounced. Most of the audience, though—the high-minded, well-educated men and women who compose the Harvard University family— felt like saying something like "I see your point, sir, but aren't you overdoing it?"*

People hunger for grandeur, but learn it's hell to live with. There are no pet albatrosses on Sutton Place, no *Curb Your Albatross* signs on Astor Street. The great are great in their own sky—in biology, stochastics, literature—but as far as the world below goes, that should be left to the rest of us. Even when "their sky" is the world, it's usually a world which no longer exists. If it *does* exist, it exists only in the heightened, purified, test-tube forms which enable them to treat it. Only the rarest of great men—Shakespeares and Einsteins, if a plural is possible here—seem not only supremely imaginative, but supremely clearheaded about both earth and sky.

Still, when a Solzhenitsyn speaks, his intelligence and bravery oblige the rest of us to listen, even if his answers are wrong or his questions out-of-bounds. For Solzhenitsyn, Western society is fearful and desperate. Its pursuit of happiness has rotted its character. On the other hand, the "hateful society" of the Gulag World produces "stronger, deeper, and more interesting characters." Of his own first day in the Gulag, Solzhenitsyn says it was "one of the best days of my life." He found there "a felicity superior to freedom itself." It's as if this great indicter of the Gulag advocates it as a training ground for Western character.**

---

*I judge from letters printed in the Harvard alumni magazine.

**Similar notions have gushed from other high-minded souls. The eighteenth-century Pennsylvania Quakers who invented what they called the "penitentiary" and who in 1790 established the first one in the revolutionary City of Brotherly Love, wrote along these lines: "Could we all be put on prison fare for the space of two or three generations, the world would ultimately be better for it." The writer, Rev. James B. Finley, chaplain of the Ohio penitentiary, was not talking about losing weight. He went on to describe "the regularity and temperance and sobriety of a good prison" which made the prisoner superior to ordinary people. (See *Memorials of Prison Life* [Cincinnati, 1851], pp. 41–42, cited in Jessica Mitford's *Kind and Unusual Punishment* [New York: Knopf, 1973].) Of course, there is one difference: Rev. Finley was not a prisoner, Solzhenitsyn was. Yet there's robinsonianism in Solzhenitsyn as

The Position of the Body

This is not the only Solzhenitsian paradox. He turns the virtues of the West inside out. The tolerance which is the essence of Western achievement, the heart of its openness to innovation and inventiveness, he calls "suicidal." As for that Western legality which is our chief guarantee of equity and justice, it is for Solzhenitsyn a poor substitute for and diversion from morality. It protects what tolerance invites, "mass living habits . . . the revolting invasion of publicity . . . TV stupor . . . intolerable music." It is hard to defend such things, yet, most of us sense that they are the price paid for a large democratic society. Since society is a kind of vast genetic pool and thus indispensable to the variety and continuity of social health, the legality and tolerance which protect it are as indispensable as the education which aims to preserve and advance it.*

2

I juxtapose Solzhenitsyn with another human being of extraordinary gift, one who, in her way, lived in a Gulag of her own, and who, like the albatross, clumsy on the human deck, is also a king of the blue sky. This is Nadia, the autistic—perhaps brain-damaged—child of a Ukrainian family who settled in D. H. Lawrence's home town, Nottingham. Nadia's family is bilingual, but Nadia, a large, clumsy, unresponsive and lethargic—if, occasionally, enraged—child, after learning ten English words her first year, lost even these. She stopped speaking, perhaps even learning. In 1971, when she was three and a half years old, her mother returned from the hospital after a serious operation. In excitement, Nadia began scribbling on the walls with a ball-

well: "It was possible for me to be more happy in this forsaken Solitary Condition than . . . in any other Particular State in the World." *Robinson Crusoe*, 1719.

*Take part in an American jury panel—as I did the summer after Solzhenitsyn's talk—and you see citizens of every sort transformed by judicial forms into sensible, responsible, high-minded jurors. On another occasion, Solzhenitsyn recognized the dignity of common democratic man: he addressed a town meeting in his adopted Vermont and thanked his fellow citizens for their hospitality and decorum. In 1985, he and his wife became American citizens.

112

point pen. Well, not scribbling. Making pictures. They were the
first positive thing Nadia had done, and her mother was delighted. The delight spurred Nadia on, and she began drawing
frequently on paper. She looked at illustrations of horses and
roosters in children's books and newspapers, and then she drew.
Not copies: she didn't refer to the placid, realistic originals. Her
results weren't limited by their dimensions or angles of vision.
With swiftness and assurance, working a minute or two at a
time, Nadia sketched her animals and people. To adapt a line
about another great artist, she "never blotted a line." Occasionally one shape would suggest another, and a second picture
would burst from the first one's side.

Nadia's general condition remained miserable. Her mother
decided to take her to the Nottingham clinic. A bit of luck. Not
only was there a well-trained, sensitive staff on call, but there
were specialists on children's art, drawn there by a nationwide
"Draw Your Mum" contest which received entries from twenty-
four thousand children. These had been collected and analyzed
by psychiatrists on the Nottingham staff. When these psychiatrists saw Nadia's drawings, they realized instantly that they
were unlike any children's art they'd seen or heard about. Indeed, there were only two or three cases of prodigious artistic
talent on record. Even these did not compare to Nadia's. The
horses, dogs, roosters, shoes, and legs which covered Nadia's
drawing paper showed a mastery of movement, perspective, and
intensity that moved Nadia into a category of her own.

The psychologists tested her. On verbal intelligence tests, she
sometimes scored zero. On artistic ones, she was in the genius
range. Dr. Lorna Selfe's book, *Nadia*, records the child's experience and progress. Nadia mastered more and more words
as she became more responsive to teachers and fellow students.
As she did, her artistic power lapsed. As of the book's publication in 1978, Nadia's drawing ability, though still far above
average, no longer exhibited genius.

I don't want to discuss the question Nigel Dennis raised in
his famous review of Dr. Selfe's book in the *New York Review
of Books*. (Namely, should Nadia have been taught anything

which deprived the world of her genius?)* Instead, I want to think about what Nadia's cry from her mental Gulag tells us.

Our time is exceptionally attuned to its Nadias, though the tide has changed in the last twenty years and children have become to some degree a despised, dependent class which scare-literature converts into bad seeds and the containers of diabolism.** Yet most Western adults still believe that a little child can lead the way. (After all, no one else has done it very well.) The art of Nadia expresses profound human hope that out of privation and misery something marvelous will come. The Solzhenitsyn who first published from the beast's belly and then escaped it is another expression of that legendary hope. But this was the old Solzhenitsyn, not the author of the Harvard address. The old Solzhenitsyn, like Nadia, had no vested interest but expression. Like Nadia, his work was a commentary on its origins. Nadia's screaming horses and roosters say something about her silence; Solzhenitsyn's cancer patients and zeks tell us as much about the Soviet world outside as about the wards and infernal circles within it.

Solzhenitsyn the artist needed Solzhenitsyn the Machiavellian. Such books as Olga Carlisle's *Solzhenitsyn and the Inner Circle* show how the artist plotted his single-handed war against the State, timing the explosions of his books, speeches, and letters so that they would hold at bay the immense forces he was describing. (It's not the first time we've seen this combination of saint and Machiavellian.)

Solzhenitsyn wants us to see a world as clearly divided as Nadia's forms are from the loosely formed world around her, but the actual world, the deck on which the albatross lands, is neither a piece of drawing paper nor the abstract model of Solzhenitsyn's speech. The artists cannot, unfortunately, control it as they can control their art.

---

*Dr. Selfe's book makes clear the thoughtfulness and humanity of the doctors who worked with her.
**Professor James Coleman has recently spelled out the awful consequences of this despised dependence for the American school system. (Edward Ryerson lecture 1985, University of Chicago)

# SCENES FROM *DOSSIER: EARTH*
## *TWENTY-FOUR BLACKOUTS FROM*
## *THE MIDDLE-ELECTRIC PERIOD*

*In late 1965, the directors of the theater at Lincoln Center, Jules Irving and Herbert Blau, commissioned me to write a play. Blau had read one of the two plays I'd written and considered it for production when he and Irving were directors of the San Francisco Theater Workshop. I'm not sure how stageworthy the play* (The Gamesman's Island\*) *was. It was considered unsalvageable by the famous Broadway producer Max Gordon. I know this because a few years before, he'd invited Philip Roth to lunch at the Lambs Club; he wanted him to write a play. Roth said he didn't know anything about writing plays. Gordon said that didn't matter, he'd had a long list of hits—he listed them—and many of them had been put into shape "by George." "Just write me something," he told Roth. "We'll let George fix it up."*

*"Who's George?"*

*"Who's George? You are out of it. George S. Kaufman!"*

*"You see, I'm not interested in theater." As a sop, Roth threw Gordon my name. "I have this friend in Chicago who's written a crafty play."*

*Gordon let Roth off the hook, and, a week or so later, I got a letter from the great man on stationery that listed his productions. Immensely flattered, I sent him* The Gamesman's Island.

---

\* Printed in *Teeth, Dying and Other Matters* (New York: Harper and Row, 1964).

*Two weeks later, it was returned with a note of polite regret
that it was not quite right for a Max Gordon production. Roth,
meanwhile, had heard by phone. "Not even George could fix
your professor's play."*

*Blau was more in my league—the literary—than Gordon's,
but he was also a theater man, so when he commissioned me to
write a new play, I didn't dwell on the fact that he hadn't produced the old one. At least—unlike Gordon—he'd seen enough
in it to believe I had some dramatic talent.*

*I wrote the play the next summer, partly in Buffalo, where I
was teaching for six weeks at the State University, and partly in
Weekapaug, Rhode Island, where I recovered from that. I sent
it to Blau, who felt there was something in it. He said he'd
schedule a reading of it in a few months. After that, he hoped
there'd be a production in the little theater under the Vivian
Beaumont. He also sent plane fare so I could look at one of the
productions and talk over the possibility of doing mine.*

*By the time I arrived and saw the play Blau had staged—it
was brilliant and exciting, but I don't remember its name—
disaster had begun to strike the theater: the unions came down
and closed the little theater and the New York critics came down
on Blau and Irving. My play was lost in the shuffle.*

*A few months later, back in Chicago, a group of actors read
through it and there was talk of putting it on. No money was
found for it. My agent told me that there was a radio performance
of it in Stockholm. Well and good, but I never saw a review or
a krona. I read scenes from it now and then to friends and one
night read the whole play to sixty or seventy people at the University of Chicago. Four of the scenes—I called them Blackouts—
were printed in the* University of Chicago Magazine. *I got a
few letters after that, one from somebody who was sending them
to a satiric cafe that was opening in New York. Nothing came
of that either.*

*Except for printing a few scenes in another miscellany, that is
the history of* Dossier: Earth. *Recently, thinking of writing another play, I got it out and read it. Not exactly my present cup
of tea, but then not a completely stale bag either. Worth perhaps*

# Wheels, Salmon, and the Jargon of Jackdaws

*one more trial flight in the world, though the flight would never again be that of 1967. What were then burning, newspaper issues are now glazed with oblivion or nostalgia. Yet the play juxtaposed the contemporary with the "historic" as it juxtaposed scenes of different sorts and genres—an episode based on the Japanese odor play was linked with a metatheatrical one—so perhaps time would do for it what it sometimes does for buildings and sculpture, supply a patina beyond the artist's gift.*

*Here I offer a few scenes in a context which—I hope—won't pluck whatever dramatic teeth they had.*

*A room of* NERO's *palace on the Palatine. Pillars open to terraces, gardens.* NERO, *26, going to fat, but powerful, cruelly intelligent, nervous and torpid by turns, slouches on pillows, picks at dishes (grapes, meat), drinks. At lights, he glances outside at terrace sun dial, golden, shadowed for midafternoon. Three servants, two pretty girls, and one pretty boy, hover around, taking dishes away at the appropriate time, fixing a pillow, getting absently stroked by the emperor.*

NERO: Sopho. Sopho.

TIGELLINUS (*a powerful, sensuous, subtle sucker-up, calls in*): Coming (*and then enters, wiping his mouth with large napkin*). Sorry. I was having a bite. (*Throws napkin to servant.*)

NERO: We augustans put some order in the days. Why are you slopping things up?

(TIGELLINUS *extends arms in puzzlement, slightly frightened.*)

NERO: It's two days after the nones and Piso's head was promised—by you—for the nones. And Seneca was due at lunch. What's *los?*

TIGELLINUS: The head's secure. Balba is on his way with it. As for the professor, when has he ever been reliable?

NERO: Don't badmouth your betters, mister.

TIGELLINUS: I'll get him myself. He was in Flaminia this morning. I'll drive the route myself. Though he's probably out of breath below us right now.

NERO: He's in better shape than either of us. A hundred million sesterces and he lives on plums and pears.

TIGELLINUS: And verses.

NERO: If I'd stuck to that diet, I'd have made Vergil look like a village half-wit.

TIGELLINUS: You've done pretty well as is.

117

# The Position of the Body

NERO: The curse of many gifts, that's Nero's life. That and imperial opportunity. Show me a genius who's free and able to do what he wants, and I'll show you a blank page and misery.

TIGELLINUS: We've had good times, *cher maitre*.

NERO: Dog brain. "Good times." What do you live for? A piece of meat in your mouth. (TIGELLINUS *laughs*.) A knife in someone's gizzard. Terror when you drive the streets. *Good times*. Life's to jump time, Sopho *meus*. I live to build. Look what I've done in the year since the fire. Instead of a stinking wooden hive of filthy pigs, we've got four regions of stone houses, fountains in every square, room to breathe, flowers, palaces, an order like grandpa's, but better, because we've got *good times*. Games instead of gloom. This is a world for quality now. You think I play like you, a pig in my own pleasure, for tickles, *good times*. I play when I'm too weak to get off the floor, for style, to set the pace, to kill the old Senecas who put black on the state and order us to fall in love with dying. I've got to reroute this straight-laced world. Rebuild it for sun and pleasure. That's what they'll remember Nero for: He took the Roman world by the scruff of the neck and led it to high bliss in the sun.

TIGELLINUS: You're a great man. Nobody denies it.

NERO: Balls. Nobody but mother saw it. But she didn't see the depth of it. That began with her death.

TIGELLINUS: Before that, sir. The golden five years of Nero began at your reign.

NERO: Oh Buster, your subtlety stops at your belly. I mean at—*with* her death. To kill the dearest thing in the world turns the key on the future. I didn't sacrifice mother for pleasure, but to kill my old threshold of pain, to show Rome it had to jump over its own shadow. Don't you think I could have handled her about Poppaea? Or anything else? You can't imagine the subtle pleasures of a mother like Agrippina. I sacrificed them as I sacrificed that filthy old town. For a new town, a new world. (*He reaches up as a girl approaches, tumbles her on a pillow, raises her dress, disappears behind the pillows. During this, a guard approaches with* SENECA, TIGELLINUS *turns, stops them at the door, holds up his hand, greets* SENECA *coldly. The room is tense till* NERO *reappears. The girl is flat on the floor; only her feet show behind the pillows. When* NERO *sees* SENECA, *he tosses a coverlet over them.*) At last, dear Annaeus. We were about to comb the streets for you.

SENECA (*subdued, sixty-four, in good shape, white-haired, simply dressed, speaks with a slight foreign accent, but purely*): Should I come another time?

NERO: Yes. For lunch. But not even you can alter the past. (*Kisses him.*)

SENECA: There are ways of altering the past, sir.

NERO: My wise tutor. Explain. No, not yet. No lectures for a bit. Something to drink. (SENECA *smiles, shakes his hand.*) Don't worry, I'll swallow a drop from every glass you touch. Or do you think the poison's in my cheek?

SENECA: You know you need no indirection to bring about whatever you wish from me.

NERO: Suppose my wish is indirection.

SENECA (*nods*): Again the pupil outstrips the master.

NERO: Not in money, I hear.

SENECA: I tried to return some of it to you two years ago. You let me know you enjoyed my keeping it.

NERO: I'm glad, dear tutor, that you've acquired the habit of remembering imperial injunctions.

SENECA: You overrate my powers as your pupil. As you did them as your teacher.

NERO: Have I failed you as pupil?

SENECA: You are the most conspicuous success in the history of pedagogy.

NERO: There was Alexander of Macedon, *mon vieux*.

SENECA: He had a much greater teacher. Considering your preceptor, your progress testifies to the powers which the slightest encouragement released.

NERO: See Tigellinus, the way men should talk to each other.

TIGELLINUS: Yes.

NERO: Go off and think about it. It's been too long since Seneca and I have had the pleasure of each other's company.

TIGELLINUS: *À toute à l'heure.*

SENECA: See you later.

NERO: We haven't seen much of each other, Annaeus.

SENECA: You have other company. (*Indicating the body behind the pillows.*)

NERO (*shouting*): Don't play with me, teacher. (SENECA *is terrified, but fights for control.*) A hole in the flesh, teacher. Is that company?

# The Position of the Body

Is that what you taught me? Is that the exchange of which Nero
speaks? Well, teacher, *répondez.*

SENECA: Inappropriate jest, sir. Please forgive me.

NERO (*the exhibitionist tyrant; quotes Seneca*): "What is there in this
world that I wouldn't do to oblige and serve my benefactor?"

SENECA: Your majesty does too much honor to your old teacher.

NERO: In dredging up your mossy saws? In quoting the corn with
which you stuffed me for eleven years?

SENECA: You grew well.

NERO (*changing*): I owe you plenty, Seneca. It's the source of much
in me.

SENECA: You owe me nothing. You owe the State, yourself, and nature
to be what you are.

NERO: No, Seneca. I was what "I am." But I go beyond that. Every
second I never *am.* I am a pile of *was's* aiming at *to be's.* What Gaius
did in madness, I've done from policy. I've remade myself, out of
your corn. It was the way to remake this bloody state. You shadow
this state, Annaeus. You're a breath of Cato's time, without his
strength.

SENECA: True.

NERO: Though you may be tempered in the proof.

SENECA (*pause*): I am ready, Nero, if you ask me.

NERO: I've been walled up by my affections, Lucius. I have been so
quick to love, and every love has brought me chancres. Mother,
Octavia, Britannicus, and you, Annaeus. Your love is bondage. Pro-
pinquity means bondage. I busted open the slummy streets of Rome,
brought in the sun, kept men apart, and now they'll flourish. I killed
what I held dear, killed myself in killing. But for liberation. It is
your turn.

SENECA: You decided this as you spoke, Nero, but the imperial whim
mortars the state. I think I know how to die.

NERO: I decide from deep policy, Seneca. I hate every day's death,
hate meat, hate plucked flowers. But the state's alive with conspiracy.
The conspiracy of the burghers, the second-rate, the half-gifted.
You're soaked in sentiment. And Rome is butchered by your pet-
tiness. I know, because half my heart is in your body. I'll stab it,
over and over, and perish with you. But I'll rot you out before I
go.

SENECA: I never knew your depths. When you were twelve, curly and
pink, you were so open. I even teased you, sent you on silly errands

120

when I wanted a snooze. You never reproached me, would go half over Rome to buy me a fish that had never been seen outside Spain, and apologize for not finding it. You were so quick, but without the least exhibitionism, just a joy in answering. I never guessed— and never have till now—this terrible capacity, never dreamt I could drown in you. Twenty years I've floated on my teacher's confidence in the answers I gave you. But you were answering questions I never knew were questions.

NERO: You have your monument, Seneca. Those first three years were yours.

SENECA: That I never understood you is my monument.

(*Noise in the background. Two guards running,* TIGELLINUS *shoots out, takes box from them, runs in the room.*)

TIGELLINUS: Sir, sir. Here it is. It's come.

NERO (*momentarily furious at the interruption, says "You—" but stops as he realizes what it is, the head of Piso. He goes to the box, his face lighting with demonic pleasure. He's aquiver, alight. The world disappears. He draws the head out of the box, holds it to his own, shudders and nods. Silence. Then*): So, Nero-hater. So, traitor. Where are all your secrets now? Look, Tigo, look (*he twirls a gray curl*). He grew gray in disservice. Ha. Poor Piso. I'll have him for supper. Invite the appropriate friends. His slut-sister. Get her from Praeneste. (*Sits on the pillows, Piso's head between his legs. Then he remembers* SENECA.) A fine friend you had here, Annaeus.

SENECA (*holding himself together*): I knew him b-b-but slightly, Sir.

NERO (*recovering*): Yes, Annaeus. The agony of power.

SENECA: It is clear to me.

NERO (*slowly*): I will clarify one more thing for you then.

SENECA: It is all clear to me.

NERO: Goodbye then, Annaeus. You missed lunch. We shall be supping on you before the Kalends.

Blackout

POPE *on balcony, blessing crowds roaring in St. Peter's Square below, out of sight, talking as he blesses to unseen aide whose voice is heard.*

AIDE: And the Portuguese group at three, your Holiness.

HIS HOLINESS: I need a longer nap, today.

AIDE: Three-thirty, Holiness.

HIS HOLINESS: Tyrant.

AIDE: Ha, ha. What for lunch, Holiness? A bit of capon breast?

HIS HOLINESS: All right, Barini. And a bit of Rothschild's brew.

AIDE: The red, Holiness?

HIS HOLINESS: If you won't leak it to *L'unità*. (*Out loud, the hand waving*): In nomine Patris, Filii et Spiritus Sancti (*intoning*). Holy Christ. What heat. How many today?

AIDE: Oh, thirty thousand, I'd say, Holiness.

HIS HOLINESS: In his whole life, the Lord didn't see a third the number. *Quel métier exécrable.*

AIDE: Holiness?

HIS HOLINESS: Sh, Barini. Go hunt up that bottle. And run me a bath.

Blackout

*Voice out of blackness, then a spot on a rifle with a telescopic sight in middle of stage.*

FIRST VOICE: Every night I go to sleep with rifles in my hand. Why? I get tired early, reading or watching television, hardly have the energy to get my clothes off, the underwear left in my pants, never brush my teeth, head groaning for the bed, strain to reach for the bedlight. Minutes after what I thought was sleep, I'm awake. Exhausted but awake and nothing will compose my mind but the rifle.

SECOND VOICE: Pistols are for suicides, rifles for other people.

FIRST VOICE: The rifle, yes. I dream it and then glide along its power. I let it speak for me. Sometimes I train it on the great. To affect the world.

SECOND: Ah, at least you discriminate. Yours is not a total hatred for the Not-You.

FIRST: Of course it isn't. I am full of love for the polloi. Elevator operators, people eating alone in the Automat, the unnamed in newspapers. No, I'm a lover. I root for the underdog, the silent assistants.

SECOND: So you have general interests and passions. What about particular ones?

FIRST: There are almost no bodies between twelve and sixty that do not derail me. Breasts stuck between a raw potato and fleshed parentheses leave me dead with want. Or dead till I strike something.

SECOND: With the rifle?

FIRST: Or the prick. It's not complicated.

SECOND: And other things?

FIRST: Elaborations. Subways, computers, input-output, hurl and fire. The rest is barrel, stock, trigger, sight, all refinement and delay. The body but a casing for that spurting continuity. That Sabbath day God rested is the curtain going up; it will not go down till everything goes down. There's only one story: Genesis.

SECOND: The rifle isn't Genesis. It's Crucifixion. Conclusion. Apocalypse.

FIRST: It's the human contribution, the artificial ending which makes the artificial drama out of total continuity. Death, thus choice, thus fate, thus beauty. Who can live without rifles? Gene-slaves. Vegetables, though what are they but green rifles? What would life be without assassins? No history, no myth, no great love.

SECOND: Does your gun ever go off?

FIRST: Always.

SECOND: Are the victims incidental?

FIRST: They are selected before the gun is made.

SECOND: Am I a victim?

FIRST: You are the indispensable recorder.

SECOND: Who is the appropriate victim?

FIRST: This one.

(*The rifle wheels toward the audience and fires loudly, whitely.*)

Blackout

*Stage mostly dark. Three twigs of light from a discreet wall lamp enable us to see a young man with long, shoulder-length hair excruciating à la suffering genius, hand to head, then head thrown back, arms outstretched, then back to tormented meditation. Nothing else visible except chair he sits in. After a minute or so, he breaks out with a furious, inspired rock chant "Ooo rahderrah-derahdeee, buhyaybee, sooteesootee bahyuhbayyybee," his body shaking, and he's up, in motion, rocking, frugging, monkeying, what have you, singing, he's flipping a tape recorder, lights, and we see no garret but the suite moderne hanging over the towers of Chicago. Our man, Norman, is dressed in the crazy elegance of post-Beatle International.*

NORMAN (*as the tune is down, he unwinds, genius exhausted*): The Gooners. (*To switches*): Nellie, bring 'em in. (*He unwinds, snapping his finger, grows sedate and the room fills, though with only five people, two advanced secretarial foxes, one black, two imitations of the boss man, ten years older, and a banker type with something besides his nose askew.*) Here it is. Rhomboid Boy-boy. (*Tape recorder on. All listen in studied ecstasy, followed by explosion:* "It it it it." "Number twelve, Normie. There. There. There. Ready. Ready." "Baby, baby, baby, baby, baby.")

123

# The Position of the Body

GEORGE: Who gets it? The Stones?

NORMAN: Gooners.

GEORGE: Riiight. Ten spot. In there. To it.

BILL (*already on phone*): Sydney, right?

NORMAN (*takes up large riding crop, points to calendar—and what a calendar—neon—points to April 16*): Melbourne.

BILL (*in phone*): Noreen, gimme Jiddley Jenks, Melbourne, Australay. What month they got going down there? Winter, summer? (*He keeps talking.*)

NELLIE: You promised the Puddlers, Normie. And they're due.

HAM (*the banker*): They got Bonnie in "Floating Tuesday." What do they need?

NORMAN: They're zip. Pure zap and zip. No body base. No roots. Motion, motion. I didn't forget 'em. Let 'em drown. "Bonny's" warping the shelves. They got a thousand returns from San Diego alone. The Midwest held 'em up two weeks. That fracture, Pelz. I'll give him air. He gets air from me.

HAM: We need him, Normie.

NORMAN: Four straight years without a loser, we need nobody. But peace. I need peace.

BILL: OK. Message. Take it. What the hell are you, baby, a shark or an operator? What kind of English you working with? Listen good now, and read it back to me. "Jiddley. Normie's got a plum for you. Repeat: For You. Fly the Gooners in Monday. We are moving." No signature necessary. Now let's hear you do it. That's right. Not bad. What you look like? OK. I'll be down your way. Sure. Spit the kangaroo outta your mouth, you're ready to go. Haaaaaa.

NORMAN: Get off the wire. Why, I let you in that Demolition riot, you were already clinging to sanity by a thread. My God, I'm working in a mangle. I can't make it here. Rudeness. People spitting in the street. Nobody washes above his cuffs. I get in a cab Thursday. "Good morning," I say, thinking I'm in a country that knows manners. This driver, gives himself shock treatment every time he shaves, says, "Who're you to tell me 'good morning'?" I got him by the throat. I forgot the world. I was squeezing his frigging gut out. Cops came up. Lucky they could see who to trust. They know these cabbies. I got out of the cab. I haven't gotten in another one. I don't care what kind of agony, how many times I get hauled off, ticketed, what, I'm getting driven in this town by my own man. That's the only way you survive in this country. You buy your own tunnel.

# Wheels, Salmon, and the Jargon of Jackdaws

HAM (*on phone*): Houston wants the Flea-boys for September. Unless the Astros win the pennant, they'll guarantee to fill the Dome.

NORMAN: OK. The usual. You think they manhandled Monteverdi? No. Musicians were servants, but servants were men. You could walk the streets without drowning in saliva. And these creeps. Putting you down. Every sixth rate Vice Pres. thinks he's a sociologist. What do they know? Social decay. What's their contribution to the body politic? Is our stuff chokin' Lake Erie? Setting forest fires? Burning the guts out of the world? They got no mind to put on the real causes, they pick on us. I've had it. In Milan, you don't get this. In Oslo, neither. London, Marseilles, even Warsaw for Christ's sake. I'm getting out. My shrink'll have to go back to teeth. What a transference. He don't even know there's a frontal lobe. Jesus. No wonder Kafka gave up analysis. I wouldn't let Freud himself put a mitt on me. No. I take that back. I'd put myself into his hands and never care about getting out. That's the trouble here. You lose all perspective. Here I'm putting Freud down with that mucking cabbie creep.

NELLIE: What about that disk for Tina Toys?

NORMAN: She's had it. Who needs her?

HAM: Come on, Norm. It's class stuff.

NORMAN: Who's telling us? Where am I? Class stuff. Get this, Hambone. That stuff is all finished. The only thing that counts now is who's in motion? Me and Cassius Ali and Warhol, we're just milk, shaked up into cream. Only reason we're visible. Nobody's around long enough to be a big cheese.

BILL (*phone has rung, he's picked it up*): Norm. You want to talk with Jiddley?

NORMAN (*reflects, rubs his eyes wearily, then picks up phone and relaxes; he's with his peer*): Jiddley, Joy, how is it there? Yeah, yeah, yeah, yeah. Happening, happening. Sure. Just for you. That's right. Right to you. Sure listen a little. (*and he does the song, swinging it out*).

Blackout

125

# The Cheepers' Shield or Making Things Up

*I cawshun'd him to keep his mouth shet and never cheep it to nobody.*
    —*Petrie, "Angeline Gits an Eyeful," cited in* Dictionary of American Regional English, *edited by Frederic G. Cassidy (Belknap Press of Harvard University, 1985)*

*Some Thracian loves the shield which I unwillingly left on a bush in perfect condition . . .*
    —*Archilochus. "A Poet's Shield"*

*This section contains brief portraits of four friends, two of them dead. All deserve better portraits, and may, one day, get them, even from me. (Warning Posted.) There are things here that should make the record though, and that will be enough excuse for printing the pieces.*

# ROBERT LOWELL

"Everything is real until it's published." Lowell wrote this as he was writing sonnets about the breakup of one marriage, the beginning of another, "absolutely writing it as he was living through it" (as a friend said). "We asked to be obsessed with writing and we were . . . " went his obituary for John Berryman, one of the other institutionalized, suicidal poets of our time. In the Soviet Union, it is usually the government which breaks, jails, and kills poets. In our country, the poets do it themselves. Why this slaughter of the comparatively innocent? Does it have to do with poetry itself, with writing down what one thinks and feels accurately and powerfully?

> sometimes everything I write
> with the threadbare art of my eye
> seems a snapshot,
> lurid, rapid, garish, grouped,
> heightened from life,
> yet paralyzed by fact . . .
> Yet why not say what happened?
> Pray for the grace of accuracy
> Vermeer gave to the sun's illumination
> stealing like the tide across a map
> to his girl solid with yearning.
> We are poor passing facts,
> warned by that to give

each figure in the photograph
his living name.

Why not say what happened?

If poets lived with cats in caves, why not indeed? But poets have wives, children, parents, friends; and poets who want to make the sort of impression on the world which will make the labels on their photographs superfluous often try to obliterate the boundary between the colorful veracity of art and the colorless disorder of life. They swallow and groan, and then they burst. They tell people off, they brawl—a word made for a poet's fights—they drink, they fall in love, they confess, and then they publish. Often their wives and friends are writers, and then there are verbal slugfests, exchanges, repudiations, retractions, reparations, consolations, pardons. Terrific stuff for poems and stories. Robert Lowell is not the first writer who used the brilliance of his wives and friends in poems. *Used*, that is, *published*, after which comes the pain of public exhibition. "I regret the Letters in Dolphin," he wrote the wife who wrote them. He called himself a shark circling his own life,

a vocational killer
foretasting the apogee of mayhem
breaking water to strike his wake.

Wives, girl- and men-friends paid plenty for the companionship of this man, but no one paid the price he paid. Within him were treacherous cells. Year after year, they took arms against the master system and broke it down. First, there'd be brilliant, unstoppable monologues, wicked jokes, then drinking and excursions along the razor's edge, new girls, declarations of new life with new apartments and crazy new purchases. A handsome, powerful, charming, troubled bear, Lowell found new girls till the very end. The end was usually mayhem, and Lowell, persuaded or coerced, entered the hospital. Mania turned into depression, then that leaked away leaving waste and humiliation, humiliation at the pain he'd caused those he most loved.

Obsessed by writing. "I feel I, or someone, wrote everything beforehand. If I had read it at twenty, would I have been surprised, would I have dared to go on?"

# The Cheepers' Shield or Making Things Up

By twenty, Lowell was already Lowell. The famous families, the acidulous, tyrannical mother, the amiable, gentle, failed father whom Lowell knocked down after a paternal letter to the father of the boy's first fiancee. He became "a case," under the psychiatric eye of Dr. Merrill Moore. (The Old Fugitive sonneteer.) Lowell was also a leader of boys, a brawler, a reader, a rebel, a poet.* Moore suggested he go south to the house of Moore's old friend, the poet Allen Tate, and later, to their old friend and teacher, John Crowe Ransom at Kenyon College. There Lowell met the literary friends of his life, Peter Taylor, Randall Jarrell, and John Thompson. He married beautiful Jean Stafford, slammed their car into a wall which smashed up her face, went to LSU to study with Cleanth Brooks and Robert Penn Warren, worked for Sheed and Ward in New York, made a "manic statement" to President Roosevelt when he received his draft notice, was jailed, came out and lived on the money Stafford earned from her novel *Boston Adventure*. He wrote, published, won prizes, divorced, remarried, had a daughter, traveled, taught, moved, broke down, moved again, broke down again, and was the most famous American poet of his time. He married a third time, had a son, then died in a taxi, age sixty, at the doorstep of his second wife.

Like many brilliant people, Lowell excited brilliance in others. If you compare his biography** with, say, Robert Caro's of Lyndon Johnson, you see the difference between history and archaeology. Unlike Ian Hamilton, Caro worked with muttered obliquities. He had to construct background out of non-literary records. There was very little said or written by Johnson or his

---

*Not unlike Edgar Allan Poe, who was described as "an imperious older boy, a capital horseman, fencer and shot and a leader of the other boys at his school in Richmond. He swam in the river James one day six miles against the tide. Devoted to music, he played a flute, he wrote good Latin verses" and so on. These poets who ended in madness had the sort of youth you'd expect from political leaders like Lyndon Johnson. Caro's biography of LBJ uncovers a sneaky, cowardly backbiter. The moral is too easy to draw. (For Poe, see Van Wyck Brooks, *The World of Washington Irving* [New York: Dutton, 1944], p. 265.)
**Ian Hamilton, *Robert Lowell. A Biography* (New York: Random House, 1983).

friends which in itself is interesting. Johnson's world was a biographical desert. In biographies, at least, the pen is mightier than the sword. Lowell's life was one of recording, expressing and transmuting facts to words. His biography, like his life, shines with the intelligence of such records, his and those of his friends.

2

A personal word. I knew Lowell fairly well. I met him in 1947 at a Carolina Writers' Conference but only got to know him in 1953 when he came to teach in the Iowa Writers' Workshop. I remember classes, dinners, rides, talk, jokes, remember his mistranslating French ("Are you sure *cil* can't mean 'eyeball'?"), playing a private charade with Elizabeth Hardwick (assigning her to do the first line of *Martin Chuzzlewit*) in the midst of our more public charades, and much else that's unrecorded in Hamilton's book. In Chicago, New York, and London, I saw more of him. (A fragment of one visit is recorded in the biography.) The point here is that a man's life overflows the most minute record of it. Like hundreds of other people, I have impressions and feelings about Lowell which aren't in these or any other pages. They aren't significant—or won't be unless I have the will, energy, and gift to make something of them—but they are a deep part of my sense of him.

Full of trouble himself, Lowell was keen about other people's. He loved gossip and was a first-rate gossiper. He was playful, analytic, allusive. The playfulness could become mean, or perhaps a better word is "wicked," which suggests sport. As a young bully, Lowell controlled with his size and fists. Older, he controlled with his tongue, and, rarely, his position (as famous poet, as a Massachusetts Lowell). Mostly, though, there was sweetness and humor, part of the honey of a nature that adored fine literary, amorous, and dramatic expression. In a life spent with writers, I've never known anyone more absorbed by literature. Books and authors were not only a consuming interest for him, they were anodynes, pacifiers, weapons. Lowell was immensely well read, far more than those whom he regarded as really learned because they'd read books or sorts of books he hadn't. He preferred reading history and criticism to poetry. In his last years, he read very little fiction. With very little gift for foreign languages he was always trying to learn and translate them. This was also true of such things as music. I sat with him once listening to Berg's *Wozzeck*, trying to follow the score. Neither of us could but both pretended to. Lowell's—our—pretense was part vanity, part competitiveness. He was a literary competitor, gamesman, and politician. (His second wife is, perhaps, the best-known literary politician in the country.) His competitors were writers who others said were his superiors. He was capable of both paying them tribute and cutting them down. (Many have developed this mean skill. Pope's portrait of Addison is its *locus classicus.*)

Because of his intermittent madness, Lowell's life had a quality certain writers who don't suffer it pretend to emulate. I believe most poets of Lowell's exceptional gift feel the disjunction between the world they knew as children and the one they encountered later and with more pain than the rest of us. Their poetry was a way of making up the discrepancy. Their verbal world substituted more and more for the actual one—at least, there was a confusion which is not present in other people—and they became part of the Great Tradition of Troubled Genius.

I once asked Lowell if his illness brought compensation in poetic insight or ability. He said that it brought him little but humiliation and a sense of waste.

Poetry, rhythmic speech, is, in my view, connected with the body's rhythms. In moments of deep emotion the autonomic nervous system takes over, the pulse of the hematic system dominates the body's rhythms, and there is often a sense of unreality. The techniques of poetry mimic and express such states. The more frequent the autonomic system is called upon to sustain the organism, the greater its sense of unreality. The discharges of endomorphins into the system to inhibit anxiety and to diminish the firing of the limbic system in the cell are perhaps the physiological equivalent of poetic pleasure. There is, then, physiological evidence for Shakespeare's identification of lunatic and poet.

# PHILIP ROTH

*I dictated the little piece about Roth over the phone to an editor
who needed it for a twenty-four-hour deadline. The writer who
was to do a long piece had done a hatchet job, crude and mean
and—what counted for the editor—boring. The writer was one
of those critics who—like a man Yeats mentions in* The Trembling
of the Veil—*conceals spite behind stupidity and always interrupts
to deform or silence intelligence. (Naturally, he's on many com-
mittees, has much power and is known as a failed this, a one-
time that, a something-else* manqué. *This makes a reasonable
dossier for a man who decides the monetary and critical fate of
others.) All right, now that's out of the way. As for Roth, he's
too good a friend to write about in detail. Yet an intelligent editor
here, a young, rather naive but literature-loving man, and therefore one after my heart, begged to know some of the inside dope
about Roth's writing habits. "You just say, 'The manuscript came
back. He'd done it again.' What had he done? How had he done
it?"*

*It's not a miracle, but it looked like that to a reader of Roth's
early drafts, one who'd argued for one sort of coherence, one
way of doing a scene, an excision here, a presence there. Won-
derfully easy to advise when you don't have to follow the advice
yourself. Roth invites several readers to hammer at his early
drafts. He's a great worrier about his narrowness, though by now
he understands he isn't narrow in the way his harsher critics say
but only severe about staying within his competence. The danger*

*in his early drafts is Jamesian qualification. His intelligence is engaged, and characters fight with brilliant primness about this difficulty or that. The wildness of his greatest characters comes harder now. That's an act that once came so easily he began to distrust it. Yet if you force wildness, it shows and nothing smells worse.*

*Roth's a great master of form, and that saves many a day. He knows when to break off a scene; his transitions are large and unexpected. Much of the formal beauty is of absence. Then too there is the beauty of persistent treatment of rich—"inexhaustible"—material.*

*Roth separates his own life from lives he creates around similar characters and events. "Was Jack Benny really a skinflint?" he asks. "So why should I be Zuckerman?"\* Right. As for Roth/ Zuckerman and the way one brings musical comedy out of the other, I can't tell the young editor very much. Omission, reduction, sharpening, that's what an editor himself does all the time. Roth also knows how to add, to invent. The rest is finding the true center of a book and leaving out the rest. That's why my little piece quotes Michelangelo's most famous technical remark. As for the treatment of self—whatever that is, as Roth worries in his latest manuscript, one whose present version is called* The Counterlife—*the Kierkegaard citation will serve as well as five psychiatric, let alone deconstructive treatments of the subject.*

"Roth."

"Schtoin."

"I took the wrong turnoff."

Every other year, I miss it. Roth is patient with his pals' lesser idiocies. For those of out-and-out fools and the laser-brained fanatics around whom his art puts bars, he's positively hungry. They're out there *living.* (Living: that heap of groans and gestures out of which he has to make sense.)

---

\*An actress friend of mine, fulsomely introduced by Jack Benny at a dinner, said, "Shit, Jack," into the microphone and was left stranded by his infuriated snub; so perhaps old Benny was a skinflint after all, but in the heart, not the wallet.

# The Position of the Body

Finally, the river, the village, the hill, the turnoff into Connecticut forest, the flat rocks, the right turn, and the beautiful double house, the eighteenth-century kitchen stocked for a weight-watcher—formerly a gourmet—siege. If you're one of the regulars, you get told—instead of shown—which upstairs room you're in. You pass the comic posters of the host: submarine-nosed, thimble-head, leaking a few black wires (done by his late pal, Philip Guston). By your bed, a pile of new books. Out of the window—lawns, apple trees, a hay field—the hostess, more beautiful than the pictures that have celebrated her since her teenage Juliet and debut with Chaplin, hanging the wash. She'll be driving to get the night's vegetables and returning for forty laps in the pool.

Sometimes there's another house guest, sure to be someone who's read and been around enough not to drop too many stitches (most of which will be in your side).

This is no vacation retreat. It's a house in which vocation and vacation fuse. The whole point is there's no vacation. Not that the atmosphere doesn't alter when a book's being started instead of finished or a play's getting prepared rather than recovered from. But Roth and Bloom, to give the hosts their names, don't store their heads with their winter clothes. They're in—as Roth says—"the same line of work," depicting human beings clearly, forcefully, and beautifully.

You don't feel inspected here, though in a house of observers, there's a certain kind of sport about this matter. Now and then something you've said or a trait you thought you'd concealed shows up on a page (or a stage). "I didn't know my head was that small."

"It's not *your* pinhead. It's mine."

People *are* noticed here, but not by reporters. This is a house of fiction-makers. Human beings in and out of the house, in and out of books, are analyzed, magnified, felt with and against so that more interesting ones can get invented. During the day, everyone's at a different typewriter; groans over misplaced commas are bouncing off every wall. We assemble at meals, breakfast and lunch at the kitchen table, Roth and Bloom squeezing or-

136

anges, cutting bread, pouring coffee. In late afternoon, it's the pool under birch trees, the trim hostess keeping trim, the rest of us on lounge chairs between the smoking insect-repellers. There may be a wrap-up seminar on the misplaced commas or a homemade routine: Roth as Olivier's Othello—" 'Now doan you say dat, Yago man, Ah doan *wanna* ring dat lil' hawnky's naik' "—Bloom finding Blanche DuBois in Desdemona.

Dinner, candlelit and silvery, is at the table in the barn. The hostess, who's cooked it—unless the host has barbecued something—is in a long dress like some queen's dream of herself. Art doesn't stop at the typewriter here. There's no snorting down burgers and Kool-Aid.

Now and then guests come from around the county or up from New York. Most are artists (playwrights, musicians, actors, sculptors, poets), people who know what it is to spend life amusing, exciting, judging, and deepening the lives of lots of other people. There's usually one conversation star per evening, seldom the same—though Roth, with a little booze in him, is hard to stop. Or rather, one wants him never to stop: There's a gas shortage, the local gas station gauleiters are rendered to the wart; then the customers get theirs, tanks and bodies open to the pump, mouths and rear ends leaking repletion. The scatological aria spins, frantic, wild, the diction lit with genial mania. Someone breaks in, there's another tack and *whoosh*, Paganini's whirling again.

The guests are off for their own beautiful acres, the home folk move to the living room for Vivaldi or *Guys and Dolls*, for a final drink and a postmortem. Or we slide back to the day's work, ten minutes become fifty, a hundred. How to get X to Y, how Conrad would do it, where James muffed it. Or where we are, what we were back in Chicago twenty-five years ago, what we're about now, what it's all about. Sometimes, despite fatigue, invention: How about this, how about that. The book's in the air, for a time it only belongs to itself, it's trying to get made, it doesn't matter who feeds it.

One summer it was *Zuckerman Unbound*. I: "Roth. To the woodshed." His workplace, two rooms across the lawn from the main house, desk, chair, couch, a picture of Kafka, the great Czech alter ego, black eyes lighting up the earth. Roth cushions his troubled back, gets out the yellow pad. "Go."

"You've messed it. The book belongs to Pepler, not the brother."

Roth writes. "More."

Speech, debate, excitement, analysis, invention, the yellow pad fills. Fifty, sixty, a hundred murderous minutes. "Don't stop. Keep going. Suppose *Pepler's* the kidnapper?"

Finally, I get out. Roth stays.

Like the great writer on the wall, he is deeply a writer. And like him also, a son, deeply, a brother, a friend—the best—a lover, a citizen and, with heavy decision, not a father. Above, beneath, and through all, a writer (whose chief subject is that). Not for self-fingering narcissism though. If anything, there's the special modesty of high intelligence, ever surer of what it can and can't do.

Eight months later, the galleys arrive. Roth, in the middle of his half-year in London—the *social* part of his life—has somehow done it again. You can hardly spot a seam—who would have guessed the pounding it took?—though that's the book's subject.

"It's simple," said Michelangelo. "Just hammer off everything that doesn't belong on the sculpture."

Or, for Roth, a more fitting quotation from one of his hundred favorite writers: "The majority of men are subjective toward themselves and objective toward all others, terribly objective sometimes—but the real task is to be objective toward oneself and subjective toward all others" (Kierkegaard, *Journals*).

# LILLIAN HELLMAN

*This piece was written shortly after the playwright's death in the spring of 1984. I'd read articles (in* Commentary *and the* Chicago Tribune*) which attacked the veracity of her memoirs, and I remembered Martha Gellhorn's similar assault. The "famous lawsuit" alluded to was Hellman's suit against Mary McCarthy's public assertion (on national television) that Hellman never wrote the truth, that every word she wrote was a lie. I cared a lot for Lillian Hellman, and I wanted to explain something about her which would be both a defense of her character and a salute to her person.*

I was in New York when Lillian died in Martha's Vineyard, had, in fact, decided to write William Abrams, who'd put a notice in the previous Sunday's *Times Book Review* asking for stories about her. I hadn't seen her since December, 1981, when I'd forgotten her unlisted phone number but done what I'd done several times before, walked the few blocks from my sister's house to hers and called through the house phone. I was with my oldest son's girlfriend, a Hellman fan. Would it be all right if I came up with her for a few minutes? Yes, said Lillian, she was all alone—the cook had gone out—and in dishabille, and she wasn't very well, but it would be good to see me and yes it was all right to bring the girl.

Her peignoir was open at the neck so that the depressed, bony triangle between shoulders and breasts, and the loose, wattled neck flesh struck me harshly. Her hair was grayer than I'd seen it, the nose bulked more than ever. It looked as if nature were sending every sort of signal to tell the flesh to give itself up.

Lillian didn't see herself. There'd been many eye operations, and she said she couldn't see much of anything. "Only shapes. I know more or less where you are."

What wasn't included in the gloomy signal system was her voice and the energy of what it did so marvelously. It began with the famous lawsuit. She'd just received Mary McCarthy's deposition. "There isn't a single instance of lying cited." What did I think of them apples? I said intelligent people had to stop talking to television interrogators as they did in their living room. The spread of domestic slander through the media would only hasten the transformation of the country into one Great Gossip Machine. This launched a story. It had to do with Norman Mailer, and it pivoted on an old sexual turndown. Many of Lillian's stories dealt with distinguished, handsome, youthful, famous, or otherwise attractive men pursuing and being rejected by her, and later taking some comic or odd revenge. This one also involved another staple, Lillian's fury. She'd hunted up "Dash's" old revolver and headed out to shoot Mailer. "Dash," the *deus ex intellectu* of many stories, locked the door and wouldn't let her out until she'd cooled off and abandoned the lethal mission.

Fatherless, guideless, Lillian had, I think, invented Hammett at least as much as she'd lived with him (and far more interestingly than he'd invented her, as Nora Charles in *The Thin Man*). Dash was the male lead in a thousand stories. He represented guidance, reason, male mystery, heroism, illness, stoicism, partnership, love.

He was not the only transfiguration in Lillian's continuous story. Those who want to nail her to the straight and narrow have an easy time of it. "I knew early that the rampage angers of an only child were distorted nightmares of reality," she wrote (just before she wrote that her story of Julia would be undistorted). How could such an enchanting storyteller tell anything straight? Aren't her plays all about inventors, liars, distorters, and fantasists? Of the sisters in *Toys in the Attic* she said, "Neither ever told the truth about anything. Not that they lied. They'd just never seen the truth about anything." Such lies are Lillian-truths: not about fact, but about the minds and temperaments which distort fact.

Many think Lillian had a life that didn't need ornamenting or transfiguring. Yet this small, dumpy woman with the great nose and flame-dyed hair had a hunger bigger than her experience, her success, her friends, her failures. She lived among great story-tellers and great drinkers, and herself knew drink as a short-cut to what satisfied her hunger. "I drank," she said, "but unlike X, Y, and Z, I got off the floor every day and went to work."

This, I think, was true. Lillian was a fantasist, but the fantasies lived off large chunks of truth. How else not be boring? She hated bores, but hated "whacks" and "crazies" even more. If she sentimentalized, it was in the direction of vividness, heroism, and passion. One night in Chicago we went out with Nelson Algren. Lillian had read Simone de Beauvoir's account of her affair with him, and this redeemed his contempt for that account and his abuse of the teller. (*His* sentimentality was never to give women the amorous time of day.) He was also sentimental about Hellman, for he'd read her dispatches from the Spanish War. Those were medals. These two fabricators enjoyed each other immensely.

Lillian loved having men around her. Some of her fiercest critics are the wives, ex-wives, sweethearts, and ex-sweethearts of the men who loved her stories and repeated them around the country. I was at her house one night when a famous Hollywood stud called her twice to report his progress with a celebrated American widow. Lillian claimed to be annoyed—bored—by the stud reports, but the fact that she was their receiver tickled her pink. (Now that I think of it, I better add my belief that the calls were "genuine.")

Lillian respected truth because she knew how hard it was to tell or take it. In fact, I think she was on the side of most of the virtues and tried to practice them. She was loyal to friends—

sitting by bedsides, taking people to hospitals—a hard worker, a clear-eyed critic, unafraid to tell people what she felt, prodigal of herself, her talents, and her hospitality. She was proud she'd earned the good life she lived, the beautiful houses, the terrific cooks, the good whiskey drunk in good company. Her compassion was genuine—the sublimation of a maternal, childless woman—and was discharged in ways that have damaged her reputation. She was wiser about politicians than politics, but most of those who call her names aren't fit to be in the same room with her when it comes to giving up time, money, and self to what she believed would rectify unfairness.

If she didn't compose her world successfully, she did compose herself. And the self I knew was pretty terrific. When I met her in 1958, she was having a rough time, didn't know if she could write any more plays, thought she might be out of things altogether. We went to see *Endgame* here in Chicago. She thought it might be a new energy in the new theater, one that was beyond her. She really didn't care for plays anymore. Still, she overcame self-doubt, and finished *Toys in the Attic*. It was a hit, and she made the money she needed. Meanwhile, in Chicago, she'd learned she could talk to college classes, and that started another career for her. Then there was the career as memoirist, the one that gave her a totally new celebrity. She became a heroine to women all over the United States. The heroine was the one she was as well as the one she invented. There was the Lillian who was the only woman taken to the front line by the Russians, who went there through Berlin (though when and how remain unclear), who sent dispatches from Spain, who wrote the sensational plays and doctored—often anonymously—such other famous ones as *A Streetcar Named Desire*, and the one who told the Congressional committee about her conscience. The Lillian behind this Lillian was Lillian, the Rememberer, the Memoirist, the Writer, the grown-up version of the girl with the rampaging anger. Lillian remembered and remade Lillian. When she wrote the stories—or when she told them—you forgot the blind little woman with mottled flesh or the warm, fluent, sometimes innocent Auntie-sort of person who said in her gorgeous voice, "Don't forget me. Come see me soon. I don't have forever."

One night in New York she said, "I thought of a title for my book today. Tell me what you think of it. *Pentimento.*"

"I don't know what it means."

"It's the sketch the artist covers up when he's rethought or reseen what he's doing. There's a secondary meaning of penitence, of repentance. Is it too fancy for a title?"

"Yes," I said, "It'll never work for you."

# COME THE SWEET BY AND BY

I have made passes at the Muse of Poetry for about thirty years. She has seldom kissed, let alone slept with me. I teach young poets. That is, I listen to their poems, say what I think about them and read them poems I like. I've seen wonderful poems come out of classes, and, more rarely, wonderful poets. For thirty-odd years, I've read poetry, old and new, and, without any gift for languages, in several of them. I've published about thirty poems, translated thirty or forty more and every year or two I write a poem or two. I have a fair ear, a predisposition for poetry with at least a shard of narrative in it, but take to almost any sort of poem. Exceptions: concrete poems, poems shaped like eggplants, poems whose trick is a comma after every word. (Does anyone else remember the, poems, of, José, Garcia, Villa,?) Most of the time, I write novels and stories, but though I haven't enjoyed as much poetry as I have fiction, I've gotten more intense pleasure from poems than stories. That's the dossier.

Seven or eight years ago, I was told about a book of poems called *Armed Love*, author, Eleanor Lerman. It took about three minutes to see what a poet this was. There were better and worse poems; that hardly mattered. The weakest poems showed a strange, strong, weirdly beautiful poetic mentality. I may have had as much pleasure reading, say, the poems of my old friend Donald Justice and a few other contemporary poets, but no book of poems took a larger jump away from the poetry around it with less sense of strain than *Armed Love*. Here was a combination of idiomatic perfection and spectral flow that hit me when I first read *"Le Bateau Ivre"* and *"Les Poetes de Sept Ans."* Indeed, Rimbaud was the poet most like Lerman. Separated by language, sex, and a century, these two somehow belonged in each other's poetic arms.* What counts in both are the intensity of the poetic I, the easy way with the familiar and the hallucinatory, the sexual hunger and estrangement, and the almost perfect ear for the entry, transition, omissions, and conclusive exaltation of the individual poems.

I invited Ms. Lerman to read in Chicago. She wrote back saying politely that she disliked giving readings and was nervous about traveling. A few months later, I spoke with her on the phone, and then one night spent a couple of hours talking with her in a Greenwich Village bar. She was extraordinarily simple, unposed, immediately human, reserved without chill, startling only in her girlishness, her *normality.* Startling, because the poems issue from an absolutely whirling intelligence, one that makes such rapid transits between the analytic and synesthizing hemispheres (I've read the topographers of the cerebrum), between fact and dream, that if her poems were recited by a person on a bus, you'd look around for men in white jackets.

Enough.

Not quite.

I've seen Ms. Lerman several times now, and we've become good friends. I've also seen and heard later poems. They are different, strongly narrative and much more straightforward. It's as if she wants the poetry to come out of the story itself like steam out of hot coffee. For these are now real stories of real people, and for Eleanor Lerman, reality emits poetic heat.**

Lerman's first book was nominated for a National Book Award. (How could it have lost?) On the dust jacket of the second book (*Come the Sweet By and By,* University of Massachusetts Press) are excerpts from professional cheers in the

---

*After reading this piece, Ms. Lerman read Rimbaud. "Not after my heart," said she. "Maybe in French," which she didn't read.
**1985. She no longer writes poetry, and is at work on a novel.

# The Position of the Body

*Sewanee Review* and the *Boston Phoenix*. The book's already been awarded the Press's Juniper Prize. So Lerman's is becoming one of the names that ring bells.*

*Come the Sweet By and By* contains forty-one poems, cousins of those in *Armed Love* and of each other, but, on the whole, deeper, more varied, longer, more complex, more worldly, more other-worldly.

For me, Eleanor Lerman is then one of the best—at least, one of the most original—poets now writing in any language I read.** And I say this without understanding—in the usual pedagogical or sympathetic reader's way—her poems.

Let me explain.

We teacher-readers are used to taking a difficult poem, "The Waste Land," say, and showing how its lines, sections, allusions, jumps, and connections belong to each other and make a coherence which can be explained in prose to someone. It's like having been in an automobile accident. After the shock, you pull what you can of yourself together, see where you've been injured, who else is, how seriously, what to do about it, how it happened.

In the case of Lerman's poems, the collision occurs, but you're thrown so far from the accident you're not even sure what kind it was. You're hurt but can't locate your injuries. If there's a phone on the corner, it takes a currency you don't carry.

The poem is, say, in a sort of religious mode. The title is "Ecclesiology," it talks of sky, starships, evil planets, necromancy, a church in Oklahoma; the five more or less similar stanzas more or less cohere about a sort of subject; so:

> germicide baths are prepared in the schoolyards:
> from one to three the female children are cleansed

---

*The bells are still. The books are out of print and few read their old copies.
**Since she's no longer writing poems, her crown passes to a number of other fine poets such as Alane Rollings (to whom I must declare a close connection) and Sharon Olds. Olds is the only poet I know in the long history of life and literature who's written directly and beautifully about pregnancy and parturition. In fact, the women geniuses of literature have, in their childlessness or *pudeur,* left an astonishing gap in our general knowledge.

146

by virgin hands, from three to five the males
At dusk the others are sent into the briar
with a horn canteen and strong soap
No one mentions the star ships
(I have saved you a plate of lichen, a crevice in the earth)

There is progress, things are picked up ("Attempts are made to shoot down the starships"), and there is a sort of solution:

a church in Oklahoma is overgrown with yellow weeds
inside, the priest walks with a stick
and has come to his grace with an infinitely tiny, rolling god
(I have saved you a wheel, a mobile heart)

But what can one say? There is a sense of beaten universe, a bit of it saved for the "you" of the poems. But far less than most poems can this one be reduced to significance. (Not that any poem is a sum of explanations. Yet almost all good poems cohere about such a sum.) Here one is content with the retrospection of a vaguely religious language situation that has been put through a subtly deranging ringer. The result is a kind of fierce farce with marvelous burnt odors coming from it. Ultimately, it is almost brutally self-contained (the indispensable, actual but never perceivable quark of Gell-Mannian physics). Except that—like a quark—it belongs to an identifiable universe, the passionate, dislocated—thank God—cosmos of the eighty-odd poems of Eleanor Lerman, a cosmos which everywhere seems to touch the cosmos of ashtrays and rosebushes, Wheat Chex and lovers but, for now anyway, as the anti-matter universe touches the material one, dissolving on touch: i.e., on explanation.

# ME TOO or ONE WITH TWENTY-SEVEN ZEROS

*Ich sage: es sind ganz besonders riechende Tiere*
*Und ich sage: es macht nichts, ich bin es auch.*

*I say: they're particularly smelly animals*
*And I say: so what, so am I.*
                                    *—Brecht, "Von Armen B.B."*

*We know the mathematical equations that govern normal*
*matter, but we cannot solve them exactly except in very simple*
*situations. Even a problem as simple as that of three bodies*
*interacting under the Newtonian law of gravity can be solved*
*only approximately. Yet the human body contains about a*
*thousand million million million million particles (one with*
*twenty-seven zeros).*
                    *—Stephen Hawking, "The Unification of Physics"*

*I threw a party, wore a very sharp suit. My wife had out all*
*sorts of hors d'oeuvres, some ordered from long off—little*
*briny peppery seafoods you wouldn't have thought of as*
*something to eat. We waited for the guests. Some of the food*
*went bad. Hardly anybody came . . .*
    *An overall wretched event was in the stars.*
                            *—Barry Hannah, "Our Secret Home"*

*Ce livre n'aura pas notre voix. Il ne parlera pas, non plus,
pour nous. Il continuera, malgré la distance, à dialoguer avec
les livres qui ont jonché sa route et dont la silence, depuis, le
hante.*

—*Edmond Jabès*, Pages d'Aely

"For a writer, shame is the equivalent of cowardice in a soldier." I think this is the Shavian quote used by one of the latest twentieth-century writers who has bared his all. (John Updike in his wonderful New Yorker essay on the humiliating skin disease which determined his marriage, his seasonal schedule and, to a degree, his literary career: "Perhaps making marks on paper removed the stigma of those on the skin.") Naturally, or unnaturally, no one bares his all. No sane person, and I'd guess, no insane one. Certainly no writer, for whom frankness is another strategy. Nonetheless, the standards of this century are such that the writer who hides within his art looks worse than the worst of self-advertisers.

The "I" that shows up in these pieces was, I think, set down without too much worry about how he'd sound. I see now that I didn't worry enough. The letters that came in after one of these pieces was published made me see what a snotty fellow I was.

I've decided not to put make-up on the body. I see a variety of me's in these small pieces. Reader, for what they're worth, take them. They were meant for you, not me. I wish I could be as pure as the creature Edmond Jabès writes about and be fed only the literary I's of others. That would be absolution. As it is, I'll learn a bit more about self-presentation by letting the I's ramble on while I listen to what the critical police have to say about them.

# INTERVENTION ON TRANSLATION

Some of my pals spend much happy time at conferences. The scholar pals read and discuss papers at scholarly conferences; the writers exchange flattery and insults at writers' conferences, read their own work and the work of ambitious writers young, middle-aged, and ancient. I've been invited to very few conferences and have attended fewer. In June, 1982, there was a rare and scarcely resistible invitation to a conference in Rome, sponsored by UNESCO and the Italian Ministry of Foreign Affairs. I'd intended to go to Spain that summer, but Spain was hosting the World Cup Football matches and hotel rooms, even the squalid caves I tend to frequent, were impossible to find. The Rome conference had to do with the fate of Italian literature in the United States. On June 1 I flew to Rome and taxied to the American Academy, the site of the conference.

Every expedition forms itself in several ways. For the attentive—perhaps the pressing—fiction writer and journal keeper, expedition-time bunches into themes. The taxi driver from the *Stazione Termini* to the Janiculum supplied the first one. A young, thicknecked, aggressively comic fellow, he was fond of very little. His chief antipathy was the Italian football team— the *Azzuri*—that was now on its way to Spain. They were, he said, certified losers, cripples who couldn't find a goal with written directions, egomaniacal cretins who wouldn't pass the ball to each other. It was clear that Italy was finished. In fact, Europe was finished. World football was in the hands of savages,

153

the Africans and South Americans. (One of my jobs is milking poetry out of such diatribes. Another is to practice the languages I have failed to master for most of my life. Though I was filthy, exhausted, and hot as a piece of stuck toast, the cabbie's assault refreshed me.) For the next month and a half, I followed the fortunes of the *Azzuri*, watched them tie the Cameroonians in a hotel at Foligno and cheered their amazing victories over Brazil and Argentina in the knickknack store below our apartment in Campo Santa Margherita in Venice. The night they won the championship, I left a Gatsby-like party at the Hotel Cipriani on the Giudecca to go to San Marco with my friend Joan FitzGerald and watch the town burst with joy.

It had been a summer of wars. Mrs. Thatcher and Prince Andrew took on Argentina over the 100,000 sheep in the Falkland Islands. Iranians and Iraqis killed thousands of each other in the hundred-and-ten-degree heat along the Euphrates, and General "Caliban" Sharon risked the soul of Israel in his punitive strike beyond the announced forty kilometers of southern Lebanon toward the streets of Beirut.

While Tardelli, Rossi, and the other *Azzuri* practiced maneuvers in Madrid, and the armies lunged for each other's throats, I was ensconced on the first floor of the Villa Chiaraviglia across the street from the American Academy. In a bathing suit, I sat in the garden, feet up on a fallen classical capital, head shaded by cypress and oleander, drinking white wine. A couple of times a day, I dressed and walked up the hill to another villa, where the conference meetings were held. There, in hot rooms, Richard Wilbur talked about taking up translation as a relief from lyric poetry, Anthony Burgess—who, it turned out, shared a birthday with me—talked about the impossibility of translating *"The Waste Land"* into Malay, Italo Calvino about every Italian writer's struggle with the problem of language. The rest of us, poets, critics, novelists, translators, chimed in with our *interventi*. An Italian conference is organized like an opera. The main speakers sing the arias, and the minor ones sign up for the equivalent of recitative: interventions. There is little give-and-take. People do not face each other at a round table; everyone comes up to the front, faces the audience, and lets fly.

154

The audience consisted of well-bred—at least well-dressed and well-titled—people, in search of guests for their own parties. In the intermissions, there was much bowing, kissing, exclamatory recognition: *"Principessa." "Ammiraglio." "Ambasciatore." "Professore."* There were also journalists, a few students, and some young scholars and painters from the American Academy. A speaker's success was judged by applause; the audience applauded most for anecdote, rhetoric, wit. My only success, a very small one, came when I told a Fernandel story about a whorehouse and a dentist. (See below.)

One man held the conference together, supplied the connections between arias and interventions, made sense of everything, praised everything, touched all bases, massaged all egos. Diplomat (Italy's ambassador to UNESCO) and scholar (Ph.D. in Romance languages from the University of Chicago), he was one of those perfections with which Italy supplies the world. His clothes were a marvel, cuffs, flaps, lapels, and pockets so beautiful that even a clothes-blind slob like me thought of visiting a tailor. The Ambasciatore's black hair and pink nails, the gold of his cufflinks and watch flickering through the hairs of his wrist, spoke more eloquently of art than any of our speeches. He summarized in English and Italian. His French, too, was perfection, and one felt that if Bulgarian, Finnish, or an African click language were needed, the Ambasciatore would supply it. The only oddity was that his felicitous summaries omitted everything which interested me. (Still, never had banality sounded so beautiful.)

In the evening, some of us went across the Tiber for dinner under a golden moon in the Campiello Lancilotti. This was life. And then there was the Pauline Chapel.

The third day I played hooky from the conference and went to see the two great Michelangelos there, *The Conversion of Paul* and *The Crucifixion of Peter.* Alone in the papal chapel with these stupefying works, I never looked so hard at paintings or felt so strongly their instruction. The painting about Peter was, I thought, about the miserable consequences of human work. It is full of picks, lances, hoes, rakes, and shovels. In its center is a magnificently carpentered upside-down cross to which the old Saint Peter is nailed. (Still, his old head is raised, and his mouth is open, instructing to the end a group of mourners.) To the right, shivering in a diaphanous garment, is—I think— Michelangelo. He's full of despair. The despair is—I *knew*—of man's work, his work of tools and weapons, of making and doing, of warfare, carpentry and, eventually, the crucifixion of the Word.

The other painting centers on another old man, Paul. He's tumbled from his horse and is half-supported by a tough soldier. His head has been struck with light. The light has come from the hand of God at the top of the painting. Everything in the painting but God's hand and Paul's face is closed. The soldiers' muscles are taut, their faces hidden; the hills are closed; a suit of armor looks empty until you see an arm and hand coming out of it; the horses' rumps face us. As for Paul's face, it is contorted with the pain of conversion. God's work.

As the third—and only living—Jew in the chapel, I felt that every would-be Pope should have to write an essay on these two great—and final—paintings of Michelangelo.

Nothing at the conference came up to them. Though it was full of delights. The last day, the Ambasciatore gave a marvelous luncheon at his duplex penthouse in old Rome. I sat with Shirley Hazzard, author of one of my favorite novels, *The Transit of Venus*, and her delightful husband, Francis Steegmuller, whose book, *Flaubert and Madame Bovary*, had spelled out for me the importance of artistic agony. On the Roman terrace there was none of that, though now and then helicopters flew close to our heads, and, down below, the streets were full of marchers and soldiers with submachine guns. (President Reagan was in town to see the Pope and President Pertini.) Above it all, we ate strawberries, quiche, prosciutto and melon, drank wine and told stories. I shook hands with my fellow *conférenciers* and walked Mary de Rachewilts to the apartment in which she was staying. She'd come up to me after one of my *interventi* and said "Do you remember me?" While I fought the cobwebs, she gave me a clue. "I last saw you in my father's house." Light broke, I gave her a kiss. It was Pound's daughter, and I'd last seen her twenty years ago. Later that summer, we went to see her in her beautiful castle outside Merano, saw her children and grand-children, the furniture Pound made, the history of China which he'd used for the *Cantos,* the antique farm equipment his grand-son Walter collected for the little folk museum established in case a Communist government came to power and threatened their tax exemption.

I saw something else that summer. A few days after leaving Merano, we were driving out of Munich. We went to see the enormous palace of Nymphenburg, and then, driving out of that pink and white nightmare of symmetry, found ourselves on Dachaustrasse. Could it be? Yes, an actual street with the actual name, and not Dachau Memorial Street (*Dachauge-dächtnis-strasse*). On the right was the Dachau Shopping Mall and there was the Dachau Housing Project. We began looking for signs to what was really Dachau, *echt* Dachau, and sure enough, small wooden plaques with arrows pointed us off the main streets and into a sort of suburban vacuum. A back road and here, a few kilometers outside of charming, *gemütlich* Munich, was a long long stretch of barbed wire, three or four strands of it with the dull damp thoughtless silver of suburban air showing through, and then, every couple of hundred yards, a beautiful watch-tower, bare with the two colors of Nymphenburg. A tremendous quiet. A quarter of a mile down was an entrance. No tickets required. Inside, a few buildings, and then bare acres. Not quite bare: there were eighty-foot-long rectangles filled with stones. Here the barracks had stood. One was preserved. We went in. Again, remarkable human carpentry. On the wall, a few pictures. The neat wooden bunks, stacked in empty perfection, were, in the pictures, packed, drenched, saturated with human beings. Heads, eyes, faces, limbs, human beings in striped jackets or bare to their fatless bodies. A washroom with wooden tubs, and was there a dining room? (I can't remember and will not look it up in one of the pamphlets I took away.) Past the rectangles was a stream with a bank of wildflowers. Beyond that was a grove with a lovely weeping willow, and then a kind of cottage, Hansel and Gretel style, except longer. And there was an extra chimney. Inside were not one but three large ovens. Also a shower room. The sign said *Krematorium.* There was more. Memorials, Catholic, Protestant, Jewish, all beautiful and bare. On a dais a book, where many signed their name and wrote messages. A sculpture, humans caught in barbed wire; a museum. Here one saw a map of Europe. By a couple of hundred cities whose names spelled out the culture of the West were black squares with other names that spelled out something else. I'd had no idea there were so many, that so many cities had these anticities, these death cities. Inside was the display of books and proclamations which charted the intellectual genealogy of insanity. It had all begun fairly reasonably, with some notion of purity and renewal. Then there were the photographs of what these notions had become, hills made up of bodies, the gorgeous faces of the lost, the faces of human beings in extremis, gouged, whipped, starved, crucified. Like a thousand thousand Grünewalds, Guernicas, or Francis Bacons, but art had not and, I believe, cannot encompass what's here. Only the facts, the documents, the black-and-white movies of the pits filled with bodies, the eyes trying to escape their faces, the immensity of the enterprise, the logistical genius of hatred.

I knew, but didn't know. As I know now and don't know. Leaving, one tried for comprehension. Did the Michelangelo painting help? Only a little. It was too grand in its singularity. It breathed redemption. Tremendous and wrenching as this memorial was, it did not breathe redemption.

A couple of weeks later, as some sort of reflex, I drove for the first time to Freiburg im Breisgau on the edge of the Black Forest. My mother's grandparents had come from here. Her father had been born here and had come to the States to marry his first cousin who'd been born in New York. I went to the beautiful, rebuilt City Hall (Red Army Faction slogans were sprayed on the walls) and asked if I could see the records of my great-grandparents. The young archivist said they'd probably be in the cathedral. I said, "I doubt it. They were Jewish." "Ah," he said, flushing a bit. "I'm afraid that all the Jewish records were *vernichtet.*" *Vernichtet.* Nothinged. "I'm very sorry," he said.

He was a young man. It was not his fault. Perhaps one of his uncles though had come in one day with an order to search out the records of local Jews and remove them from the files. Who knows why? Did the pieces of paper infect those near them?

There was more to the summer which began with the *Azzuri* and the drive for the World Cup and had gone on through General Sharon's and the other wars, past the Michelangelos in the Pauline Chapel, but for me the summer ended there in this beautiful town on the edge of the Forest where undoubtedly the men and women who'd passed their leg shapes and eye colors down to me had gone for walks and swims and bicycle rides, but had not left any paper trace of their births, marriages, and funerals.

(*What follows is my "intervention" on translation, transcribed and cleaned up.*)

It's not easy to speak after Soldati and Burgess. I feel like a janitor at the circus or the man who sweeps up the stage after the curtains come down on *King Lear.* The morning has offered a debate about translation. On the one hand, translation is seen as a bridge, on the other, a form of treason, not just the betrayal of an original text, but the importation of a subversive text into an alien culture. Most of us would say that such subversion is the essence of culture. Yet, occasionally, translators, cultural bridgebuilders, are seen and even treated as traitors. (I think of those famous prisoners and exiles, Ovid, Raleigh, Saint Paul, Ezra Pound.)

Let me offer two stories to illustrate the extremities of the translation problem as I see it. The first has to do with a proposal made in the 1930s by the great Beethoven pianist Artur Schnabel. Schnabel suggested that only German pianists could play Beethoven correctly. At the time, Mr. Schnabel lived on 86th and Central Park West and I on 84th. Although I was half a century younger than he, he occasionally suffered me to walk with him. After his proposal came out in the *Times,* I was perturbed enough about it to ask him if it might be that only pianists from Bonn could really play Beethoven. He laughed that off, but to me his thesis reduced to this: not merely Bonn pianists, but those who lived on Beethoven's street, maybe in Beethoven's house, *and* during Beethoven's lifetime, could play him correctly. In the end, only Beethoven himself could play Beethoven. With such reduction to the absurd, the limitation of Schnabel's thesis was clear. Culture is interpretation, culture is diffusion, culture is translation. Limit interpretation and translation arbitrarily and culture collapses.

The other extremity might be expressed by a famous routine of the great comedian Fernandel. One day, Fernandel decides to go to a brothel. He runs to the building, but, in his haste, gets off not at the fifth but the fourth flour. The fourth floor is a dentist's office. As Fernandel waits in the anteroom, a man enters, muttering, "Don't know why I come back here. Last time, they took mine out and put in a gold one." Fernandel's famous equine mug registered the appropriate horror and his audience collapsed with laughter.

Many of us have read glittering translations which may have looked remarkable in themselves but which were useless as translations. Indeed, I would like to recommend the translation Susan Sontag* commended, Nabokov's four-volume Pushkin, for the Fernandel Gold Tooth Award.

I suppose the ideal translator should be like Bernini's Saint Teresa, ecstatic in receptivity of the great text from on high. But the fine translators in this audience (Steegmuller, William Weaver, William Jay Smith, Allen Mandelbaum, and Richard Wilbur, among others) know there are other motives than Teresian ecstasy behind translation. Even hatred can motivate translation. If Sartre had translated Flaubert instead of writing four thousand pages about him, I suspect you could see that his motive was the desire to substitute for every Flaubertian atom an atom of himself. Richard Wilbur has spoken about the origins of his great Molière translations: they exist because Wilbur found himself unable to conjure up a second voice of his own. How lucky we are that he was dissatisfied with his limitations.

A word about Calvino's remark that every Italian writer lives in a state of linguistic frenzy. ("What sort of language shall I

*a fellow-*conférencier*

160

use?") With all respect to Calvino's knowledge and literary power, I wonder if a writer like Moravia worries as much as a writer like Gadda, or if Tozzi, Svevo, and even Verga* or Dante struggled as much about language as Calvino himself. There have been and probably always will be the writers who work from the text of nature (or *imagined* nature) and those who work from verbal embodiments of nature. The most influential of all translations—the Bible—suggests in Genesis that creation began with nature, but in the fourth Gospel, creation is said to begin with *the word*. Philosophy has struggled with the relationship of word to what is worded. Writers take their own stands here. Some of us believe that ours is the old Greek job of representing powerfully what we have seen, felt and imagined more or less powerfully. Others feel that the act of representation itself is the proper subject of further representation. Does the word invent what is there? Or does it transmit, transform, translate, mimic it?

For those who focus on the Logos, translation represents a double hazard. Sometimes the writer is bold and gifted enough to translate his own work (Beckett) or employ a son/daughter to do it (Nabokov, Pound). Sometimes he supervises a team of translators (Joyce). The great King James Bible was a group translation. (As if divine fecundity had inseminated several Teresas simultaneously.) Calvino says he likes to work with his translators; Sontag wishes her Hungarian and Japanese sontagifiers would ply her with questions. I'll conclude with my own very limited experience; the only times I've worked with a translator of my work, I not only learned more about language than I have in any equivalent span, I learned more about the workings of the work itself than I could have in any other way.

*October, 1985. Calvino died last month. At the Ambassador's party, he took gentle issue with my remarks. He said Verga had indeed agonized about what language to use.

# ANSWER TO A SYMPOSIUM QUESTION

Dear Jonathan:

   In brief response to the overwhelming questions: the political issues are what they've always been: (a) equality of opportunity obtained without massacre and (b) the collective enterprise expressed not by terror and bellicosity but by projects of exploration and creation. The insane allocation of the world's wealth confirms every pessimistic assessment of humanity. The technology of information offers the hope that human relations can proceed along the lines of equity, yet we have always found a way of getting in our own way. The power of modern weapons and our insane accumulation of them almost persuade the rational person that he's part of a diabolic force, that he's seeing the inorganic taking its revenge on human exploitation of it. The "death wish," the drive to dissolve into component elements, has been discarded as an interpretation of collective process. The artist, more than most other humans, goes against the grain of the collective in order to register whatever in him differs from others. By being true to everything in himself that has not been expressed, he becomes a part of the expanded collective, but while he works, he works against its grain. To some extent, he serves to absorb some of the energy which would otherwise express itself in meaner ways. The artist is most political, most social, and most moral when he is being true to those insights and feelings which in themselves are apolitical, asocial, and amoral. He deepens and subtilizes human possibility which

counters hatred and anxiety, broadens tolerance, and reem-
phasizes the human need for equality.

Yours,
Richard Stern

# THE GLASS GODDESS

A few years ago, a student of mine wrote a story about an erotic encounter with Linda Yu, then a reporter and anchorwoman for Chicago's television station WMAQ. The encounter was imaginary, but nonetheless it surprised me. It didn't occur to me that the pretty teamsters of the news penetrated viewers' consciousness deeply enough to star in fantasies and dreams. The stars of my own erotic extravaganzas were real stars: Rita Hayworth, Alice Faye, Virginia Mayo, Elizabeth Taylor. Occasionally flashing meteorites wandered in from the pages of *Life*. How could a Linda Yu star in a genuine fantasy? It's clear I wasn't watching television news as much then as I do now or I would have understood its invasive power.

Happiness combines novelty and familiarity. Every day the same: boredom. Every day different: unbearable. Every group has its own threshold of novelty. In 1800, Wordsworth was dismayed that people hungered for hourly news bulletins. Two centuries later, people consume a diet of novelty that would have driven their ancestors into the madhouse. Editors of newspapers and television are thermostats of news-delivery systems. Their job is to know how much worldly change we can take in an hour, a day, a week. They also know that shocking news must be delivered in non-shocking ways. News must be a *digestif*, an intermission of sanity from the world's percussive furor.

Night after night, week after week, year in and out, the mostly young newscasters (wonderful words recalling Millet's *Sower*) not only bring bad tidings, they sweeten them. They're like the croissants Mme. Verdurin eats while she sighs over the horrors of war reported in *Figaro*. Familiar voices, white teeth flared in enchanting smiles, fine clothes, reliable syntax, easy intercourse, all soften the abductions, rapes, murders, tornadoes, the bombs, plagues, and crashes we ingest with beer and burgers in excited repose between work and sleep.

Walter, Ron, Floyd, Max, Mary Anne, Susan, Carol, Deborah. In Chicago, thousands of people welcome their faces and upper torsos as intimates.

With a difference. Walk down a street and bump into a friend and your smile evokes his. This is real affection, two-way intimacy. But if, by chance, you run into Ron or Walter, Susan or Linda, shopping at Field's or eating a frank at Comiskey Park, it would be like running into Zeus. You'd glow with the thrill of recognition, but they would not. If, by some miracle, your smile would ignite theirs, it wouldn't be because you were recognized as an individual, but only as the familiar, dazzled spectator out of their sight behind the electronic curtain.

Incarnate gods evoke powerful, passionate, and awesome feelings in those of us consigned by fate and talent to be anonymous dots in the cast of thousands. Yet the more crowded the world, the greater the distance between such gods and their devotees. Buddha and Jesus walked the ordinary streets. Papal representatives don't dare. Even protected by guards and special glass, they risk assassination. In the 1790s, President Washington received any citizen who wished to pay him a courtesy call. Today a presidential reception is an affair of state, and a presidential burp is interpreted by ten thousand sages. The occasional closing of the gap between the world's stars and their fans makes some of our favorite stories. The deranged Londoner who got past Buckingham Palace guards to end up on Queen Elizabeth's bed one summer morning can only be topped by so sinister a version of the story as John Hinckley's attempt to offer President Reagan's corpse as a gift to the child actress Jodie Foster.

Most stars—political, cinematic, athletic, religious—know that at least in public they have to be charming, even seductive. They

165

caress us with smiles, wit, and sincerity. They appear to deliver up their lives to us.

Yet of course they can't; there just isn't enough of them to go around; and what there is needs—even more than adulation—repose.

To some degree, we all play roles in the dreams, fantasies, and lives of other people. Psychiatrists make good livings out of the distortions of such role-playing. Years ago, I was pursued by a deranged girl who'd once typed some fiction for me. She'd put herself in place of one of the fictional characters and believed I was sending *her* special messages through the text. She elaborated fictions of her own in which I was alternately hero and villain. Even from the institution in which she was eventually placed, she called me with cryptic messages of love and hatred. For me, too, it was no joke.

Another bit of personal history. I sleep and rise early. For the past few years, part of my waking routine is taking cereal and tea in front of the six twenty-five news. A few years ago, a new news face appeared on Channel 5. It was that of a fine-featured girl with blond hair. The girl had a wonderful smile but did not smile gratuitously. She delivered her three or four minutes of news with seriousness, rapidity, and clarity. Her expressions suited the story, no easy matter in the emotional smorgasbord of the business. This precision and beauty were slightly flawed. Occasionally the face was poorly made up. The full lips were over-lipsticked, the golden hair was goofily coiffed—or un-coiffed. Often the girl's clothes seemed bizarre. She wore a lot of white, and this during a Chicago winter. All in all, though, I was taken with her. I knew that when other newscasters showed up at 6:25 and my heart fell. I missed this intelligent, slightly hickish beauty.

She had a name out of a nineteenth-century British novel or a 1940s MGM film: Deborah Norville. I told others that Deborah—one calls fantasy pals by their first names—was the best newscaster I'd seen in a long time. One of my sons is a print reporter. I told him I was sure this girl was going to be a star of the news world. (He's a dear son and doesn't do much loud

166

disagreeing, but he was less sure than I.) In a few months, Deborah turned up as an anchor on the five o'clock news. Her usual partner was and is an intelligent, agreeable man, Ron Magers. I followed Deborah as a snake his charmer's flute and made the difficult switch from my old favorites, Walter, Don, and Johnny.

In a real relationship, beauty, like other virtues, merges with personality and character. Only rarely is it isolated in the lover's consciousness. The beauty of our Fantasy Intimates remains up front because it is what we know, that is, what we see. Of course we hunger to know more, as we do about our analysts, our bosses, our professors, our presidents. We relish every tidbit dropped between invasions and basketball scores. Of Deborah I learned she was from Georgia, that she loved sports, that she had a grandmother who made dolls, and that she was, though clearly intelligent, not a person of broad or deep culture.

The lives of our fantasy creatures are in a way manipulable. Cathy Crowell Webb said about the story she wove about her imaginary rapist, "Since he didn't exist, I could make up anything I wanted to about him." For Deborah, I didn't do much inventing. Since my business is fantasy—that is, inventing stories—I'm more careful about it than most people. I was content to take her as she was, a pleasant part of the day's routine.

I enjoy talking to strangers in foreign trains and buses, but I tell myself I'm practicing the language and picking up details for my work as a storyteller. I also have a special interest in exceptional people, and now and then I've overcome timidity to seek them out. When I was eleven or twelve years old, reading *Arrowsmith, Main Street,* and *Babbitt,* I spotted Sinclair Lewis in Central Park, and though I saw him move quickly away as I approached, I trailed and cornered him, and proceeded to ask questions about his books till he got rid of me. About the same time, my parents were surprised to see me walking down Central Park West with Artur Schnabel. (They did not hear me ask him if he'd like to use our piano; he told me he had one of his own.) For a while, I wrote heads of state asking if they wanted me to write verbal portraits or take down their dinner conversation.

# The Position of the Body

On the most beautiful stationery I've ever seen, the secretary of a secretary of Winston Churchill informed me that the prime minister's staff was complete. In later years these fits of pursuit have usually come when I've finished writing a book. I start hunting around for new projects, preferably some which are a relief from invention. Recently, then, after finishing a book, I decided one thing I could do would be to explore this one-sided intimacy between those on different sides of the television screen. The decision was connected to a desire to meet the lovely Deborah. In any event, I wrote her solemnly about "the project" and after a few delays, and just about when I'd started on three or four other things, we met for lunch.

2

No better place to probe essentials than Chicago. A winding river, looping trains, buildings high, low, square, round, domed, turreted, steepled, made of fifty kinds of opacity and crystal. Inside, every imaginable sort of human commerce. The sun falls out of its thermonuclear heart and turns glass into fire, copper into mirror, river into silver. What counts is *Now*. What you hear is noise; what you see is motion: internal combustion, pneumatic drills, the thrust of buses, boats, trains. Whatever is salable is sold. *Selling* itself is sold; "futures" are sold.

We met at The French Bakery, a restaurant tucked into the main corridor of Chicago's greatest hive of selling, the Merchandise Mart. In stone, the princes of American merchandise glare into the building: Sears and Rosenwald, Field and Filene, Woolworth, Ward, and Wood. Divine septuplets of commerce, icons of this great gray bulk which the Bostonian manipulator Joseph Kennedy bought for twenty-five million dollars in the twenties and which gave him the nucleus of his fortune. (Without it, would Camelot Two have been?)

I'm neither selling nor buying. I am, I think, inquiring, an older man's version of courting. Deborah arrives on the dot. (TV people, like geniuses, are always prompt.) She wears a black cloth coat, a long-sleeved grass green blouse which ruffles around her long, lean frame, a calf-length skirt, and boots. Her first words are her name, snapped a bit nervously as if on a roll call. Beauty should be a passport to ease. It isn't, but at our back table, we're soon at ease, she with Diet Coke and chicken salad, I with the dull Chablis of an average business lunch. I say, "I hope you won't mind if I ask a lot of questions."

"That depends on the questions," she says wisely. Why should she give herself away?

Yet that's what the citizens of the Age of Openness are supposed to do. Never have so many given so much to so many. With this kicker: since we're expected to deliver our selves, we deliver them in prefabricated boxes. So, never have so many sounded so much like so few. Starlets, sculptors, pitchers, punters, magnates, musclemen, statesmen, and madmen answer standard questions, and sound more or less alike. (Now and then a child or, more rarely, a genius of veracity—or mendacity—sounds different.) Pigeonholes are also hiding places. Everyone has much to hide. The interviewer's job is to pull his quarry out of one pigeonhole and put him in another. As for Deborah, I believe she hoped that I would make an attractive pigeonhole for her. (I don't think she'd been interviewed very often.) Nothing wrong with that. Everyone likes to see portraits of himself.

Portraiture isn't easy. Nor is two hours enough to probe a mind, let alone a character.

I found out a little. Deborah is a child of television. As a teenager—or was she even that?—she saw the actor Michael Landon at some televised festival near her home in Dalton, Georgia. From then on, she wanted to have something to do with television. At the University of Georgia she majored in broadcast journalism. One summer she wrote news copy and advertisements, did reporting, editing, and broadcasting for a local radio station. In her sophomore year, she was hired by an Atlanta television station. A sorority girl, a cheerleader, a Junior Miss, a perfect 4.0 student, Deborah had a second life in television. Like her Indiana-born mother, who ran a business when she was twenty-five, Deborah was off and running in a career when most girls are dreaming about dates. The career was almost magical. Wherever she was, Deborah was *spotted,* sometimes by a passing executive, sometimes by an executive's wife. She went over to the CBS station in Atlanta and then, three years out of college, in the terrible winter of 1982, up to cold Chicago at WMAQ.

As for home-life, that too was an idyll. Like the popular Warner Brothers films of the forties, the Norville household had four daughters, all close, all successful. (All but Deborah have stayed home, married and built houses close to each other.) A lovely family then spawned this lovely princess.

Of course, golden bowls have their fault lines. (These were the plots of the *Four Daughters* films and *The Golden Bowl.*) Her parents divorced when Deborah was fourteen and her mother died six years later. A small puzzle. Was Deborah telling me or herself that life had been more or less perfect?

I'm a great life-fool myself. That is, I form scars quickly and either jest or cover them out of existence. An American trait, this, the basis of American transcendentalism. Emerson and Whitman are its bards, Hawthorne and Melville its enemies. As for Debbie—she referred to herself this way—perfection seemed a slightly perfervid pitch. Yet, after all, compared to what she sees and reports, her life had been golden. Arsonists, murderers, rapists, molesters, and their victims, these are her daily fare. Atlanta's pudgy—her word—child-killer, Wayne Williams, had been a stringer for her Atlanta station. (She feels that played a part in his ability to attract his victims. "Our TV wagon would pull up and kids would crowd around it.") Chicago has an even richer supply of imperfection than Atlanta. A week earlier, Deborah had gone into a filthy tenement where a family of five lived. They'd had a priest as boarder; he'd slept in the bedroom, indeed the beds of the three sons, and had eased himself on their bodies. Now he was in prison, and the family, deprived of his rent money, was starving. It did not make the newscast, but it had shaken Deborah; as did the fifteen thousand members of NAM-BLA whose motto is "Sex before eight or else it's too late"; as did the catalogue of naked children offered to their customers. Day after day, this lovely girl dips herself into such cesspools.

Yet here she was, cool, blond, charming, fluent, as free of taint as the sun on what it shines. I could see why she lit up when sportscasters talked of the orderly violence and controlled assault of the Bulls, the Bears, the Cubs, and the Hawks. She seemed to take exceptional pleasure in such competition. I think I understand this. I too get wildly involved with fights, tennis matches, the Cubs and the Bears. I get involved in order not to think about other things. They are for me what Harlequin novels are for others. The confrontations are clear, the ups and downs are naked, there's enough of a mental component to engage more of you than, say, eating a hamburger, and then there's the sympathetic mimicry of physical engagement. No wonder active statesmen "relax" with sports. And no wonder that Deborah relaxes with them, for she too is in a very competitive world where, in a minute, you can disappear from the glass screen. No matter how comfortable she may feel "on the air"—and my guess is she feels as comfortable there as she does in her bathtub—she's still where she can make the kind of mistake that could end her career.

I asked her if the ring on her third finger meant she was married. She flushed a bit, said it really wasn't a *wedding* ring, just a ring. No, she wasn't married, nor did she now have a "deep attachment." This left her free to go elsewhere, if the right elsewhere came along. No, she wasn't looking, she likes Chicago, likes her work, likes almost everyone she works with, feels she's liked by them. However, she's still being spotted. "They considered me for Diane Sawyer's job. Very flattering." As for replacing her WMAQ predecessor, Jane Pauley, "Jane's doing just fine."

Deprecation, irony, sportiveness, all this and more are on the Norville palette. A certain southern courtesy and deference as well; very attractive to older types like me. If anything's missing, perhaps time will supply it. Intelligence, analytic power, energy, good work habits, emotional suppleness, all these Deborah has. Is it mean of me to say I felt something missing?

I see more and more intelligent young people for whom the classic schemes of reference don't exist. They pick up, they shortcut, the old currency isn't in their pockets, they don't even fumble for it. When I told Deborah that her family reminded me of those in Jane Austen, I sensed a blank in her face. When she said she'd tried to read Bellow's *Him with His Foot in His Mouth,* but it had puzzled her, there was a blank in mine. (Till I realized that Bellow's comedy would only register for those who have lived and read long and well.)

The pedagogical and erotic parts of me wanted to take this girl in hand. The erotic part I reluctantly threw into the generation gap. As for the pedagogical part, my desire to tell this girl what I knew felt too much like the compensatory labor of a failed courtier.

Deborah knows the vocabulary and syntax of her world better than I know mine. She delivers the glitter of her world and glitters herself. Did it matter to anyone but types like me that some old comic wisdom isn't part of her life?

We'd been sitting almost two hours in artful dimness. It was time to go, and she was off, a tall, slim, full-chinned, Viking-belle of a girl, rapid, efficient, self-contained, sweet, well-mannered, and then, like everybody else, ultimately mysterious.

3

André Malraux wrote about the effect of modern photographic reproduction on actual works of art. The enlargement of detail, the spectacular illumination of facades, the dramatic juxtaposition of ancient and modern works, make for a sensationalism with which the actual works can't compete. Viewers trained on reproductions are often disappointed by the dullness of the originals.

Something like this had happened to me with Deborah. Home, three hours after our lunch, I watched her *do the news.* There were the green blouse and the blue eyes of the restaurant. In the restaurant, though, the light was crepuscular and Deborah was life-size. On television, especially in close-up, the eyes were immensely blue, heartrendingly lustrous, appealing. In a way,

Deborah was closer to me here than in the restaurant. Not entirely. Her television voice was cheerier and somewhat blander; the irony and sharpness of the restaurant voice were self-censored for the tube. Then, too, in the restaurant, there were the small unvisual currents which pass between living creatures, waves of heat, pheromones—skin-fragrance, perfume—and there were, as well, the shifting tension and security of a *tête-à-tête*. On television, Deborah's lines were fluent. In the restaurant there were some pauses. Some of what we said was pat or, in my case, pedagogical and pompous. In short, it was a mixture. If there had been a possibility of a developing relationship, the restaurant meeting would have been much more exciting than it was. There hadn't been and it wasn't. So there was a slight flatness in our farewell.

Driving back along the lake, I did not feel the stuff of an essay in our meeting. Nobody had said anything memorable. I liked Deborah, she was a charming person, delightful to look at and listen to, but that was that. When, a few nights later, I listened to the English physicist Stephen Hawking lecture about time, I knew immediately there was a real subject here. Hawking suffers from Lou Gehrig's disease. He rolled himself on stage in a wheelchair. In it, two useless legs were crossed at the knee. Above the twisted torso was a squarish, eyeglassed head which reclined on a headrest. Out of his mouth came strange, whining sounds, like those of a wounded animal. A young English graduate student somehow managed to translate this whine into crystalline sentences which were linked to each other with beautiful rigor. This made for a real story, maybe a modern version of Philoctetes, the only man who could draw the bow of Ajax (whose equivalent here was Einstein) but who suffered from a wound so purulent that he had to be sequestered (the Hawking equivalent was his disease). But what was the Deborah story, The Glass Goddess and the Old Voyeur? Hardly even that?

I felt guilty at having wasted her time. I wrote her a letter of apology, offered to introduce her to a nice young philosopher I knew, asked if she'd like Swedish translations of my novels for her relatives in Göteborg, told her sagely that wasting time was good for people and that I hoped she'd waste a little with me again someday.

Wisely, again, she didn't answer. I continue to watch her on the five o'clock news. I enjoy seeing her cope with Ron and Warner, John and Jim. When she goes out on stories, it's nice to glimpse her full-length and in action. That some of the bloom is off the rose is my own fault: I should've known I couldn't go through that magic glass.

# THE DEBRIS OF A NOVEL

As I've finished the novel,* it's time to get rid of the paper which underwrote it: early drafts, notes, clippings, dictations. There are piles of them, a foot high here, two feet there, on the radiator, the window sill, above books, above records, under the stereo. The University Library collects my papers—a Minor Amercian Writer of the Mid-Century—so I call Special Collections and say there are too many pages for me to haul over myself, could they send help? "Will one box be enough?" I think so, but when a man arrives with it, and we start stuffing in the pages—there must be four thousand of them—we see it isn't. I find a couple of paper bags, we carry the mess down to the car, and I drive it to the rear entrance of Regenstein Library. There they go, my life for five years, paragraphs written in 1979, deboned, remade and fused with those written last week, whole sections of books I didn't write. (Can they be saved for other novels?) There are ten or more versions of an African chapter, at least as many of a Roman conference. Characters, scenes, sentences, ideas of every sort, gone into the archives where, perhaps, some curious student of the twentieth century may one day get a clue to the spirit of the times, or, at least, to its literary pathology.

I haven't felt the usual relief or exaltation. This novel has cost too much. There was a sort of happiness at the final rush: the

---

*An earlier, much longer version of *A Father's Words* (New York: Arbor House, 1986) which turned out to be unfinished, or, at least, unpublishable.

decision to use the five 1979 pages instead of the overactive African chapter was, I think, right, and only took three more drafts to get it about right. That made for a nice feeling at the end, a bit quiet, but then, that's what the book is, quiet. The hell with noise. I'd read the last Updike novel (*The Witches of Eastwick*) the weekend before I finished the book, and it had troubled me. So much in it. He really gives you your money's worth: the fine sex of the delightful witches, his Father Mapple-like sermon on parasites, the pages on the Bach Cello Suite. (His new wife must be a cellist.) He really does supply things, but then, the embellishment is unremitting, and five percent of it, anyway, works against the book. I hear he's bought a word processor. What will this do to literature? He must be trying to displace every other book in the stores. Between him and Joyce Carol Oates, the language will exhaust its supply of sentences.

Word processors, though, have been at the back of my mind. Why should I have to truck over this mountain of literary garbage? Why not something clean, something that wipes out the *Schmutz* of ink blots, Liquid Paper, early thoughts, fragments, drafts, false directions? I've told myself I'd look into it, and that afternoon I do.

I run into a colleague, a linguist, Joe Williams, who has had a word processor for years. He invites me over to see his. We go up and down staircases and corridors to his office, where, on a table, is a keyboard, a small glass screen, and, on the window sill, the gray slab which is his printer.

Joe is intense, bearded, eyeglassed. He adores his computer. "If someone would tell me 'It's either this or your daughter,' I'd have to think twice. The first two weeks, though, were a nightmare. They nearly broke me. The thing changes your style, changes everything, but now, I can't live without it."

He sits down, there is tension in him, a pianist about to play the first bars of the concert. He puts a small record—a soft disc—into a slot and says "This is the program." Below it, in another slot, he puts an identical disc. "This is what I'm actually doing." His hands jab—no, *touch* a few keys. It is very quick, and the screen lights up with code words Joe's made up to stand

176

for his activities. There are lots of them, twelve or fifteen different things with which he works. I tell him I want to work with only one thing, writing.

"Fine. This is a Kaypro Two. You should probably get a Four. It'll give you about sixty double-space pages on a disc."

He touches the keys. The program asks him what he wants to do. He makes a new entry under "b-stern," and types out, "I want to show Richard something about the computer. He's had no experience whatever with one." Then he shows me how he can change words, insert phrases, *justify*—that is, *align*—the text on the left and the right.

"How about seeing it on a page? I like to feel the words there, like to scribble in the margins."

He yields to my antiquity and presses directions for printing. Oops. Something's wrong. "What an embarrassment. In two years, this is the first time there's been a snafu." He writes up another text: "It will be humiliating if you screw up while I'm boosting the machine to Richard." This works better. The slab on the window sill chatters a few seconds and Joe tears out his sentence. The original sentences of "b-stern" are lost somewhere in the machine. "I wonder if it means this isn't meant for me, Joe."

"Once you try it, you'll never go back. It's a Strad instead of a cigar box."

No doubt there's virtuoso delight in the machine. I remember my first days driving a car. What power. What ease. I can also imagine the temptations of virtuosity. But what do they have to do with my enterprise?


2

I wouldn't mind changing the way I write. After all, I just did that with a book. I dictated most of the novel. Five years ago, I got an assistant, an intelligent, sympathetic young woman, Susan Albertine, who not only got all my words down in the right order but laughed, groaned, and responded in other ways. I tried writing stories with her. It worked out pretty well. In a year, I finished a book of stories and much of another "orderly miscellany." Then I started dictating what became the novel. Never had so much come so fast. In a few months, there were a few hundred pages, a few of them interesting. So easy. You just took off. OK, there were days when it was hard to open your mouth, but you always did. After all, Susan couldn't be expected to just sit there waiting. That wasn't sociable. So almost always there was something.

What there was was a novel about two men, Riemer and Firetuck. One had been everywhere, the other nowhere; one got involved with something called the Farce Movement; the other went on doing his work as the editor of a science newsletter. The idea was to involve the quiet one in the schemes of the adventurer.

I went off on an African tour. Susan helped me prepare the speeches, some in French, which she knew well. When I came back, her time with me was nearly over. She had to do what Albertines do, disappear.

Heartbreaking. I began with another assistant.

In the next three years, there would be seven of them.

The new assistant was younger, less literary and less expressive than Susan. I had to spell out words for her, and when the texts came back, the sentences were wrong. She hadn't caught what I was doing. What should have been periods were commas; the beginning of one sentence turned up at the end of its predecessor.

In addition, the young woman had a speech defect. One of the book's main characters lisped. I eliminated the lisp and then the character. Then I eliminated the assistant.

Another came, a good-humored, intelligent, portly woman. In a few days, she'd picked up my prose habits; paragraphs came back the way they'd gone out. Bravo.

But here too was a problem. One of my characters was fat and made savage comments about other people's fat. Once again, timidity held me back. (I could dictate "fuck" but not "fat.")

By now, the book had bigger problems. I cut out Firetuck and the Farce Movement. Things went better. But it was May and my portly assistant graduated.

Now I was used to dictating; I got another assistant. This one had no sense of any language, let alone mine. "Sorry," I said. "It's not working out." That was the only sentence she understood.

In the fall, I found a graduate student in music with a first-rate ear for prose. She came three days a week. I prepared for her the other three. In seven months, I had a draft of the novel.

A disaster. It took six weeks and a critical friend to make me realize it. What had happened? Was it my dictatorial squeamishness? The change in auditors? The different pace? Or just me?

After stewing in misery for a month, I began again, but in the first person. This helped, though it meant changing almost everything. Everything but the rhythm of dictation. Apparently, this novel belonged to dictation, as Mozart's melancholy belonged to G minor.

3

The night I finished it, I had the following dream. I was employed as a defuser of bombs which exploded when unauthorized persons entered safe deposit vaults. The owners of a vault died. (The dream associated them with an American couple who'd deposited a fertilized embryo in an Australian cryogenic bank.) I was ordered to defuse or detonate the bomb. I entered the vault with a hammer. There were roars of objection to the crudity of this "detonator." "I know," I said, "but it's all I have." And on I went toward the vault.

My dream ended with an interpretation of itself. It turned out that the valuables in the vault were the lives of the people I most loved. The bomb was the dictation of the book which dealt with their transformation.

What did the dream have to do with the book? A great deal, but the pertinent question is "What did the dream have to do with the way I've described the book here?" The answer to that is "very little."

The point is that the core of the book was never Firetuck, Riemer, and the Farce Movement. The heart of it was—is—a transfiguration and projection of the author's relationships to two wives and four children. The miscalculations, waste pages, skewered drafts, the four thousand pages in the archives of failure have far more to do with the failure to see that than with the misdirections of dictation.

I think I'm finished now with family novels. I've hurt everyone I can hurt. Not—as far as I know—trying to hurt, but there it is, and I paid for it with the thousands of pages, the thousands of hours wasted, the typed excursions to Africa and Tulsa, the hearts and pockets of inventions I'll never use. I was punished for failing to see my subject. I must get another. No amanuensis and no word processor will make that easier for me.

# UNDERWAY

I doubt that there's ever been a totally naive literary act. The very manual energy involved in the transfer of thought to paper is at some point entangled with awareness of the process of transference. To some degree, then, there's always been what Henry James called "the story of the story." *How did this poem come about? How or why did I—or he—write this? What is the relationship between the words and the actualities or images to which they seem to refer? In what ways are this text and this author products of economic, political, social, sexual, linguistic, literary, and other ventriloquial powers?*

The twentieth century may be the great promoter, distributor, and advertiser of such questions and their answers. That so many modern writers make their living teaching alongside scholars and critics has not impoverished the literature of narcissism.*

2

I'm going to add my bit to it here and now. There's some danger here, I know: "Never seek to tell thy love / Love that never told can be." There's some law of diminishing returns at work when a force retracts for self-regard. Mine will be partial, what John Ehrlichman called a "modified, limited hang-out."

---

*That it may have impoverished literature is another matter.

One alert. I'm not going to put much psychological pressure on myself. That deep fears and desires determine the shape and content of books is no secret. It's probably best, though, that they remain secret to the author-sufferer.

One guess: work which involves complex choice is best done by people whose selves are up for grabs, people, that is, whose egos need lots of bolstering. I don't know if the author of "When in disgrace with fortune and men's eyes" had a fragile ego, but I suspect his extraordinary work was not just the spume of a cyclonic personality. His famous sweetness and just as famous litigiousness are, I think, signs of an exceptionally tender psyche. (Now I'm going far beyond the caution I intended; it's clear my own tremulous ego will go to any length to armor itself.)

## 3

> Die angefanen Skizze zum Roman—mit der Kindheits-geschichte voran—ähnelt im Schema den Vehwirrungen.
> —Robert Musil, *Tagebücher* (Rowohlt, 1983), p. 71.

> Autobiography is a particularly deceptive form of deception.
> —R.S.

It isn't easy tracing the origin and elements of any fairly complex complex. One of my weaknesses makes this particularly difficult. In the past ten years I've had trouble screening out what belongs and what doesn't to the work in progress. I think I've felt that with time growing short, I'd better deal with everything I know.

I write this piece three months after dispatching the galleys of a work which I mistakenly had thought finished in 1983 and again in 1984. In Regenstein Library there are several thousand typed and scribbled pages, a monument to this literary sickness of excess, indecisiveness, and bad judgment.

Now I'm engaged in another literary civil war. When did it begin?

4

Beginnings. Much tougher to describe than endings. All right, you get *the idea*—I won't bother working over this complexity—an idea that looks as if it'll stick. (Again, I won't analyze the thousand whys of that.) Even one of Poe's ideal lyrics is made up of more than one idea. Pinning ideas—or inspirations—down is not easy. The road to Slobovia—the motel version of Xanadu—doesn't pass through gorgeous country, yet it's every bit as tortuous a road.

Yet there is a road, and though, like every other, it leads not to Rome but the Big Bang,* it does stop at similar destinations. In other words, every discussion of beginnings is more or less arbitrary. One just says, "Here."

This discussion is different from most in not being after the fact. Not only has the trip to the novel hardly begun, its destination is uncertain. All I can say is that it's novel-bound. I'm sure I'm carrying too much baggage for a short story, even a long one, and my gifts exclude epicwriting.

5

In the spring of 1982, my friend and former student, Jim Schiffer, invited me to talk at Blackburn College in west-central Illinois. I took a prop plane from Meigs Field on the lakefront to Springfield. Jim met me there and drove me sixty miles of corn-heavy prairie southeast of Springfield to Carlinville. This small town, the site of one of the Lincoln-Douglas debates, centers about the college. Its outstanding building is a Greek Revival courthouse which in 1870 had cost a million dollars and caused a scandal. Early in the century, a seven-foot seam of coal was discovered under the town. It was bought by Standard Oil of Indiana, which then purchased through the Sears, Roebuck Catalog fifty or sixty pre-fabricated houses for the mine work-

*Which, if I follow Stephen Hawking, is itself not the Ur-state of Being.

183

ers. Seventy years later, these gave Carlinville a little burst of publicity.* There is little else to draw national attention there.

By the time Jim put me on the Springfield plane the next day, something about the town had started to work in me. The people who came to my reading, mostly Blackburn students and faculty, were so lively and attractive that I felt as if I'd come upon a new link in the great chain of human culture. Out here on the prairie there was this eagerness which, a century and a half earlier, had brought out a Lincoln.

There was another feeling, reminiscent of one I'd had more than thirty years earlier when I'd first driven through Europe. Driving through Spanish villages I felt Zeus-like. Zeus moved at will through a static world, picking up, then returning whatever charms and goods he wanted before moving on again. Somewhere between the sense of the great transmission belt of culture and the sense of Carlinville's small, manageable, static remoteness was a desire to write about it.

I grew up in New York City and have lived most of my life in Chicago. I've written mostly about city people. Even when my characters live in small towns—as I have now and then—they are in retreat, or exile from the city. Now, I thought, there's something I can do with a small town. The fact that I know very little about living in one is, if anything, an advantage. It'll allow me, it'll force me, to invention. The danger is that I'd fall into the inventions of other writers. I have to be careful to avoid the versions of Anderson, Faulkner, or Flaubert.

I needed my own handle.

In the summer of 1982 I found one. In Venice, I met a middle-aged American who, unlike most Americans there, was neither an artist, a scholar, or a millionaire. Jim had grown up in a small Iowa town and fallen in love with Europe through reading Hemingway and Fitzgerald. He quit high school, left home, and got a job in a shoestore. At eighteen, he was drafted and sent to Italy. Immediately he knew it was where he wanted to live. He also knew that a foreigner with no degree and few skills couldn't

*Smithsonian Magazine, November, 1985.

survive there. He decided that after his discharge he'd go home and save enough money to retire in Italy. Back in America, he worked in shoestores all over the country, California, Arizona, New York, Ohio. Then, with a fifteen thousand dollar loan, he opened his own orthopedic store in Flint, Michigan. In ten years he sold out, repaid the loan, and invested his money in tax-free municipals. Then he took off. Later, back in Italy, he realized that he'd miscalculated inflation by two-and-a-half percent. Now in Venice, he counters the discrepancy by renting rooms to visiting American graduate students, professors, and artists. It's turned into a double boon, for it's given him the sort of company he prefers.

Jim is the basis for my character, George Share. George doesn't live in Venice or want to.* George does work ten months a year in his own shoestore, but his life there is shaped by something else, something I came upon a few weeks after I met Jim.

I was driving in the Jura. It was a wonderful day. I kept getting out of the car to smell the mountain air. In a village, I picked up a hitchhiker, a girl of nineteen or twenty who worked for a jeweler in Les Chaux-des-Fonds. I asked her about her life—she was too polite to ask me about mine. She said she loved movies. I said that people had been telling me to see a film called *Tre Fratelli;* I'd tried to see it in Chicago, Rome, Venice, and Munich; just that morning I'd read the paper in Basel to see if it were playing there.

"I've seen it," she said. "We have a *Ciné-club* at home." (The population was eleven hundred.) Her high school history teacher had started it five years ago and showed its members the best European, Japanese, and English-language films.

In Willsville, George Share starts such a club. At home, he has a library of classics and good new books. There, too, he hangs reproductions of paintings, sculpture, and buildings. For

---

*I'd decided that George would be different from his model before I'd read a Somerset Maugham story about an Englishman who saves money enough to live ten years in Sicily and then, when the money runs out, dies—with a smile on his face.

twenty years now, Willsvillians—mostly young ones—know they can see the films, borrow books, look at paintings and discuss them while they drink Chablis and eat good cheese. For twenty years, George's house has been the social and intellectual center of the county, and for twenty years, George has taken the brightest and prettiest county girl to Europe as a sort of graduation present. The novel opens in Venice during the summer of 1982. George is living in Campo San Margherita with Bug—real name June, nickname "Junebug"—Venerdy, who discovers in the course of the novel that the first Willsville girl awarded this European diploma was her mother.

## 6

Every once in a while, somebody in search of a lecture topic berates American writers for not dealing with great public subjects and men in public places. There is, they say, no American equivalent of Asturias's *El Señor Presidente* and Garcia Marquez's *Autumn of the Patriarch*, of *War and Peace*, *The First Circle*, *Lucien Leuwen*, or *The Charterhouse of Parma*. The only American writers who write about men in high places are popular writers like Upton Sinclair, Herman Wouk, and Allen Drury. (I think Wouk's versions of Hitler and Roosevelt in *War and Remembrance* are more interesting than Solzhenitsyn's Stalin or his Lenin in Zurich. The reason may be that, lacking imaginative power and a dominating thesis, Wouk leaned on good documentary material.) As for the Latin-American works, they derive from a political and literary tradition of grotesquerie and farce. (Farce is a traditional way of handling grotesquerie. American writers from "Sut Lovingood" to the authors of *Macbird* and *The Public Burning* have responded to their sense of political grotesquerie with the same weapons.) There are, however, no American versions of the political characters in Stendhal, Tolstoy, or Trollope. That's the vacuum I'd like to fill.*

---

*I speak of a literary vacuum. American films and television dramas are full of presidents, generals, senators, and cabinet ministers. The usual dramatic

## Me Too or One with Twenty-Seven Zeros

Like most people, I've spent most of my life far from the corridors, let alone the seats of power. Men and former men of power come to the university, and now and then I meet and talk with them, but that's about it. In that same summer of 1982, the secretary of state who replaced Alexander Haig was a former colleague of mine. I'd not exchanged more than a few words with him but I did know his new deputy and many of his friends. At last, a foot in the door of the mighty. I felt an itch. Even though I think the point of fiction is to make the "unimportant" "important," I thought, "Why not relate the man I know to the public product of which he is an ingredient?"

Until a novelist like me fuses personality and theme, there is no fiction. As for me, personality almost always requires setting. As if to aggravate the new itch, my daughter moved to Washington. Her husband actually works for the State Department. Things were conspiring in a fictional direction. As for Washington, unlike Willsville, it didn't have to be invented. Its actuality is so rich it's as much as a writer can do to handle a thousandth of what he sees there.

In the spring of 1984, then, I went to Washington.

When I went into the deputy's office in the State Department, I saw him looking at the television news broadcasting the first electoral returns from El Salvador. He said U.S. observers would be flying back to Washington at three, they'd report to the president at four, and a statement would be prepared for the

---

strategy is to make a political step personally costly to the protagonist. So a president's wife will be in the town he has to bomb. Movies have done better with farce (*Dr. Strangelove*), as the theater did with musical comedy (*Of Thee I Sing*). The basic message is, "You think this is crazy? Go read the *New York Times*."

Then there's the treatment of great men by greater men. For Sophocles and Shakespeare, the rules were different. Oedipus and Hamlet have personal problems, which means that the states they rule—or should rule—have them. This was the case for early novels as well (*The Tale of Genji, The Princess of Cleves*). In the last two hundred years, the state has outgrown personal britches. (This was true even in Stendhal's little Duchy of Parma.) The novelist should treat a public figure as he'd treat a grocer. The business counts—competition from a supermarket or a superpower—because it transforms the protagonist's life, not vice versa.

187

media at five. "It's not the world I worry about," he said. "It's Congress and the media."

It struck me that he had a problem similar to mine. He had to make sense of a large complex of events for somebody else. He is a charming, witty, and intelligent man, obviously at home in the world which reduces the pains and pleasures of several billion people into manageable abstractions. (I want my "man of power" to have some of his range and charm.)* He and his wife took me on a brief tour of the seventh floor. Much of it is a museum of American art and artifacts. There are American versions of the great furniture makers, Sheraton, Hepplewhite, Chippendale, and the Adamses. There are Philadelphia high-boys, Shaker chairs, satinwood commodes, teak secretaries, Boston rockers with spiral arms;** there are fine porcelain jars and tea seats of Lowstoft and Wedgwood, beautiful paintings by Marin and Childe Hassan; there is the double-tiered desk at which an upright Jefferson wrote the Declaration of Independence. The rooms breathed symmetry, reason, and beauty. I imagined diplomats from Zaire and the Seychelles walking to appointments here and sensing the America which grew not out of intolerance and mass murder but out of the eighteenth-century Enlightenment, an America of equity and beauty. Whoever surrounded American power with such works of art had done something wonderful.

The deputy secretary's dining room is called the Livingston Room. We ate under a portrait of this diplomat who'd nearly haggled away Napoleon's gift-sale of the Louisiana Purchase. (There's a marvelous account of it in Henry Adams's great history of the United States.)

I asked my friend if anyone in the State Department had time to actually think about foreign policy. He said that there really were a couple of people around who did that. I said I'd been

*March, 1986: I've just had an extended lunch-talk with another old friend who is Undersecretary of State for Economic Affairs. Once again, I felt the intellectual and emotional range—tragedy to farce—of international affairs.
**March, 1986. The Undersecretary told me this is the finest collection outside of the one at Winterthur.

reading about Spain—I was going there that summer—and was struck by what had happened to it in the centuries following the discovery of the New World. Gold poured into the country, prices were inflated, human energy went into speculation, into ideologies of national purification, and then aggressive armament. There was also the cultural flowering of the *siglo de oro*, but this marked the end of Spanish greatness. Ruinous engagements were followed by a four-hundred-year slide into parochialism, strife, tyranny, and a long national snooze. I wondered if there were a lesson there for us? My friend had neither time nor inclination to discuss this. The most he ventured was that our Central American policy had a great deal to do with fears of Americans in the southwestern states that they'd be overrun by Latin immigrants.

To get to the point here: I was fascinated by the literary possibilities of men like my friend, the deputy. And soon I saw a connection between their international world and George Share's *école des femmes*. George too had foreign affairs. Now he was going to have something else: a brother who like him had left Willsville, but by another route: the local college, then the University of Chicago Law School, a Wall Street law firm, and, finally, the State Department.


7

I began doing more political reading than I usually do, and it was through a book that another element of the novel's matrix entered. The book was Daniel Ford's *The Button,* a discussion of nuclear strategy which reinforced the feelings of dismay and farcical *je-m'en-fichisme* which grips me when I try to understand large-scale politics.

More importantly, the book generated another character. Ford describes the strategic notion of *decapitation,* the policy of eliminating enemy leadership in the initial nuclear strike. The Soviet Union and the United States take various measures to deal with it: they have alternative headquarters within easy reach of their capitals (though nobody has figured out a way of communicating

The Position of the Body

from them in an atmosphere of nuclear explosion). The Americans also have Looking Glass, planes in the air twenty-four hours a day commanded by general officers supplied with communication codes to unleash the counterstrike.

*My* counter to decapitation was this: the National Security Council assigns some general officers to various parts of the country. They bury themselves in little towns accompanied by the codes which enable them to destroy the other half of the world. *My* character ranks number thirty-two in the hierarchy of succession. He is sent to Willsville, where he buys the town's grocery store. A hundred feet below its crates of tomato juice and crushed pineapple is a concrete room containing the communication system which will insure that a half-incinerated America will incinerate its incinerator.

As I read the Ford book, I also read a story in the newspaper about several owners of midwest pizza parlors who turned out to be Mafia moles. They'd been placed in small towns years ago as drug distributors. My grocer-general, now in his ninth year in Willsville, is a good friend of the local pizza parlor operator.

So the theme of the double life, already present in George Share's ambivalent tutelage, is reinforced.

Now I don't want to write a Jules Romains novel, one in which an entire town is dominated by a single phenomenon. (I think he called such dominance *unanisme*.) My interest remains the psychological and dramatic pressure which makes individuals go different ways. So my decapitation hero's wife disintegrates under the duplicity of her life, and one of his two daughters becomes Bug Venerdy's successor.

There are many other things which I see going into this book. I'll mention only one. My wife worked as a rental agent in a large apartment complex. Her colleague was a fine young black girl who was unjustly accused of stealing a master key, threatened with prison, and made to take a lie detector test. The girl resigned and so did my wife. In my book, I make someone like my wife the daughter of the State Department official. (Which makes him older than my friend, the deputy.) He is used to—and occasionally charmed by—his daughter's letters of protest about foreign policy. Her views are as changeable as mine often are. In life, this is awkward. In fiction, it's a godsend. (Any continuity full of ups and downs is a dramatic and psychological goldmine.)

A few words about literary considerations which, at least indirectly, shape this novel's matrix. I've grown tired of the domestic subject matter and sedate prose which have been my stock-in-trade. I've read work by such writers as T. Coraghesson Boyle, Barry Hannah, and Thomas Pynchon. I like their energy, allusiveness, obliquity, obscenity, and—looking at all of them— the range from articulate mumbles to Joycean polylingualism. I don't know how much I can alter but I hope this novel will be invigorated by my new admiration.

Some recent French critics indict most American writers for textual naiveté. They claim that Americans don't make linguistic and narrative subversion the center of their work. For me, narrative naiveté is essential, and, at least until revision, stylistic naiveté is essential also. My energy goes into the construction of a story which seems beautiful and moving to me. Language is, of course, a powerful component of the beauty, but I do not engage it immediately as Mishima claimed Japanese writers engage Japanese and Italo Calvino claimed Italian writers engaged the problems of their dialects and Italian. Nor do I wish to make such engagement the center of my work.

## 8

A final note. Over the course of writing a book, one's feelings go all over the map. The relationship of extra-literary to literary feeling is a wonderful subject.* Here I only want to say that the feelings which dominated my life before I started thinking about the book were a sense of waste and a sense of dangerously pleasurable comfort, both of which I consciously related to preparation for ceasing to write (and, for that matter, ceasing to live). Feelings pivot on very small happenings. Think sadly of X, and

---

*I've had a whack or two at it in my non-fiction books: *The Invention of the Real* and *The Books in Fred Hampton's Apartment*.

a delicious nostalgia soaks you. A dream evokes a scene which overwhelms you the next morning. To some degree a novel is affected by powerful new feelings, but, after a bit, the novel-in-progress acquires an emotional life of its own. More and more it's insulated from other events, other feelings. It has its own rhythm, its own principles, its own ranges of thought and feeling. This novel is not far enough advanced for that. My fear is it may be dying even as I write this. That is, it may not yet *be* an "it." Of course, my hope is, as I said at the beginning, that this abstract preview will not be its epitaph but a part of a fructive matrix.

# STATEMENT FOR THE AMERICAN ACADEMY
# AND INSTITUTE OF ARTS AND LETTERS
# (May 15, 1985)

> " . . . a short statement on your work in which you
> might describe your working methods; plans for a
> future project; your thoughts on the current award;
> autobiographical anecdotes; or any topic you find
> appropriate."

Work. It's unfair to call some of it work. Work is what you do. In the best times, something is done to, or within, or maybe even despite you. This often happens in those no-place hallways between sleep and waking.

Then there's the time of perfect liberty. Alone in the small room with the dictionaries, the typewriter, the shell ashtray, and the rectangle of Chicago sky, you leave all this for the Great Boundlessness. It's there you meet the choices which become your work.

That these choices have been so paltry is the first and worst disappointment of this retrospect. That all you've seen and felt and been, all that you've pretended to be, all that you've imagined, all the nuttiness and wildness have come to so little seems pathetic now. The inefficiency. The waste. The dumbness. The cemetery of pages. Typed, inked, penciled, arrowed, x'd, hexed,

193

piled. Each other's tombs. (Yet kept, for who knows when you'll find a gold filling there.)

What isn't buried, what's on show, is a couple of thousand pages, a dozen books or so which testify as much to fatigue and abandonment as triumph. Awfully small potatoes for those thousands of hours in the field. (Was the soil punk or were you?)

The prize. Totally unexpected. Out of the unblue blue. Strange, beautiful, heartrending, disturbing. The last because you'd settled into a version of yourself which excluded such acknowledgment. You protected your vanity by telling yourself you'd renounced it. Better to be an anchorite than a constantly rejected suitor. (After all, deep down you knew you didn't deserve the girl.) So that's what kept you going. And it was *going*, it is going, not resignation that you want, the pleasure of telling stories, of setting things straight, of praising, punishing, surprising, laughing and making "them" laugh and cry. Making sense and nonsense out of everything, disentangling life from bad words, making it clear in your words.

The prize has been given to some of the marble statues in your pantheon; yet you know there's nothing marble about you. Unless it's a mistake, a joke, you've got to deal with that. You look at biographies to see how the statues received the award. A bit surprising. In 1949, Thomas Mann wrote "Dear Archie" (MacLeish): "It has been said . . . that I, more than any other writer, consider myself worthy of any distinction, received from the contemporary world." Nothing, dear Archie, can be farther from the truth. "I've just muddled through . . ." and "This is the greatest honor my American colleagues . . ." and so on.

Dreiser, Auden, Odets, Hemingway, Huxley, O'Hara.

Hemingway's plane had cracked up in Uganda, he'd read his obituaries, but, months shy of the summons from Stockholm, he's thrilled, delighted, enchanted, as he spends the award money over and over with epistolary pals.

As for that tough guy, John O'Hara, he bursts into tears; he's been denied so often, been belittled, ignored, shunted aside. This is "the climax of my life."

Can it be? Are there marble tears? Or is the stock of human reaction so small that tough guys and tender ones, giants and pygmies, feel the same way?

So what do I do? What do I make of the award? Use its fine, small music to make a graceful exit? Or, since what's outside that exit looks like the Great Boredom, can I somehow buckle myself into this armor and see if it won't give me a little more courage to go further into the Boundlessness than I've gone? That would be a prize.